A DIM WORLD

VOLUME 3

THE GREAT FORGET FANTASY SERIES

TERRY IRONWOOD

All rights reserved. No part of this publication may be reproduced, stored or transmitted in any form or by any means, electronic, mechanical, photocopying, recording, scanning, or otherwise without written permission from the publisher. It is illegal to copy this book, post it to a website, or distribute it by any other means without permission.

COPYRIGHT © 2024 by Terry Ironwood

THIS NOVEL IS ENTIRELY a work of fiction. The names, characters and incidents portrayed in it are the work of the author's imagination. Any resemblance to actual persons, living or dead, events or localities is entirely coincidental.

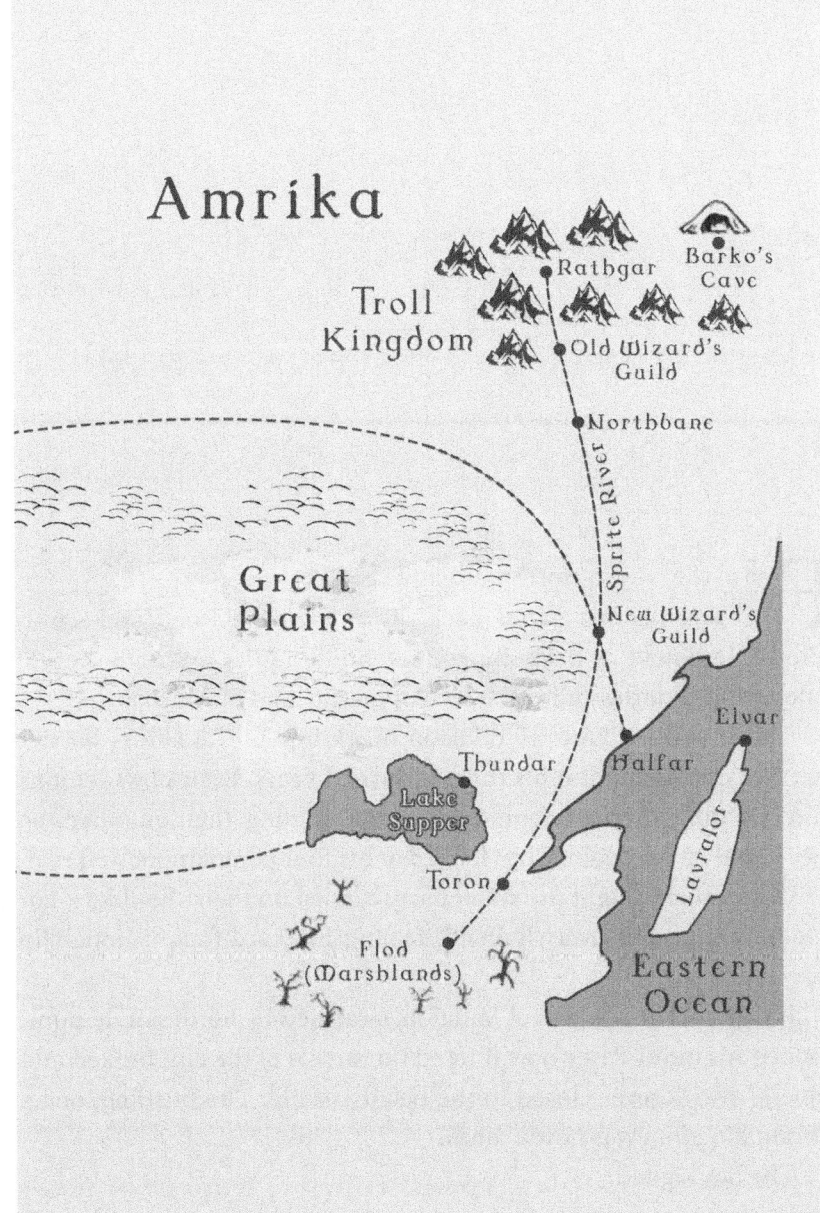

1

F ar to the west, a storm was gathering.

The orphan gazed back down the One Road and shuddered. He knew a dark force was building its strength before unleashing countless hordes of evil upon the land of Amrika.

The Unnamed One would soon break free of the failing barrier that had contained him for three thousand years. Even now, demons were slipping through temporary rifts, building their numbers so they could attack again. Chip looked at his four companions and realized how much weight the small party carried on their shoulders. For a moment, he felt overwhelmed, feeling his hard-fought hope slip away.

Images of the soldiers of Vanalon, swarmed by hordes of demons, flooded his mind. They now littered the streets of the city, broken and lifeless, eyes forever closed to the beauty of life. The bustling, once-vibrant kingdom was now a tomb.

The boy sighed.

He knew that their sacrifice must never be forgotten. Despite terrible losses, they had defended the city, stalling the demon's advance. He was grateful for winning the battle but knew the war was only beginning. Chip took a deep breath and cleared his mind, remembering his lessons on positive thinking. He must live in the moment.

The Grey Mountains surrounding Vanalon rose like majestic pyramids on either side of the One Road as the companions continued east.

They caught glimpses through the trees of the mighty Rocky River, which accompanied the road to the Great Plains. The sun rose above the peaks, bathing them in warm autumn air. The leaves on some of the trees were already starting to turn from bright green to vibrant red and orange.

The air smelled of fresh pine with slight hints of wood smoke coming from the sporadic homes still holding occupants. The others were left vacant as the owners followed the fleeing Vanalon citizens to the safety of Calgar.

Chip took in the surroundings, allowing a smile. He had never left the city of Vanalon. His life had consisted of school and training for so long that he frankly was not sure there would ever be more. He still held the memories Xander had shown him when he was a young boy of exotic places and fascinating people. Chip treasured those memories even though they were not his. As time went on, they seemed like wistful dreams that he would never experience.

Now, he rode east with the people he cared about most, and every sight he gazed upon seemed full of new promise. His optimism suffered when he glanced at the princess and saw her haunted eyes. She had lost her father to a demon assassin and her brother, King Rupert, to the evil General Morgo. The orphan held no love for either but knew all people had some good in them. They did not deserve such a fate. He held her reigns and slowed their horses to drift behind the others.

"Are you all right?" Chip asked with concern. She nodded slowly, looking into his green eyes. He reached out and wiped away a tear that ran down her cheek. "I'm sorry for your loss. Your brother had no love for me, but he was able to put that behind him leading up to the battle. I respect that and wish things had turned out differently. We lost so many lives. I'm happy you are safe."

He leaned over and hugged her as the horses came to a stop. She squeezed him tightly and buried her face in his shoulder. Hearing her weep struck a deep chord in his heart, and he vowed always to protect her.

Chip could hear the others slow their mounts. No one said anything. It was obvious Eleanor needed time to grieve. The battle with the demons had pushed them all to their limits. The boy could hear the weapons master admonishing him in his mind for believing limits were real. Even so, they had been tested sorely and welcomed the time to heal, grieve, and reflect.

Princess Eleanor lifted her head, and he felt her lips brush his ear. "Thank you," she breathed, sitting upright and taking a deep breath. She looked at the others gathered a short distance away. "Carry on," the princess called, forcing a regal smile. "I will be fine. It really is a lovely day."

Chase dropped back and rode with them, calling out some of the sights. Chip saw Eleanor glance at them with a smirk as the gawking boys pointed animatedly and chattered back and forth. He knew she had been to Calgar several times before for royal visits and even once to the capital, Toron. Chip, satisfied she was in better spirits, immersed himself in the sights and sounds of his surroundings. She had always wanted him to see new things and experience more than the mundane life of the keep.

The party moved at a brisk pace despite their weariness. They had been through a lot in the last couple of days and still required much rest, but their mission was urgent. The companions briefly stopped to eat bread, cheese, and fruit beside a part of the Rocky River near the road. Swimming in certain areas along the One Road was safe but treacherous when the river narrowed or went over rapids. The villagers knew the safe spots for swimming and the best areas to fish. Many folks had single homes dotting the small lakes, and some were still fishing and swimming. Several asked them for news as they passed by.

Xander's message was always the same. "Leave for Calgar while you still can. They will provide you with food and shelter. The demons are real and coming. If you insist on staying, flee with the Calgar army when Vanalon falls, but it might be too late," the wizard spoke the words gravely, leaving little doubt. Some villagers, of course, would never believe it. Chip sighed, knowing they couldn't save them all.

The companions stayed on the One Road for the remainder of the day. They made small talk and the wizard seemed content to allow them all a respite from the recent events so they could experience the beauty of nature. The light-hearted talk was frivolous, with frequent bursts of laughter. Even Garth shared in the occasional smile.

The sun was beginning to set behind them as they approached the tiny hamlet of Deer Run. It looked almost deserted. Many houses had boards over the windows indicating the residents had heeded the warnings and moved their families to safety. Light from oil lamps shone through the shutters of other homes, indicating they still had occupants. Smoke billowed out of a few chimneys, dissipating into the darkening sky.

A dog barked in the distance, announcing their arrival. Xander directed them to the middle of the small town, where a smoky light shone out of the only inn. An outside sign read, "The White Deer Inn and Tavern." The smell of roasted meat wafting from the entrance made their mouths water.

"We can dine and rest here," the wizard said, tying off his horse to the front railing. "Until we hit the plains, there should be little fear of observation. Those with loose tongues would see us riding through anyway. If any ask, we are citizens of Vanalon making for Calgar. Princess, I request that you don your hood while we are inside. There is a chance someone might recognize you."

Xander had switched his blue robe to a plain gray one after lunch. No one needed to know he was a wizard of great Power. Garth raised his hood and covered his weapons with a cloak tied at the throat. He told the others to adopt the story that they were a family who worked at the keep performing various duties. They had fled the city to escape the demons.

The inn's front door was wide open, so they walked through to a large common room. It was half full of villagers and travellers. The latter sported backpacks or belongings held close. A family with three children had what looked like most of their worldly possessions surrounding them. Xander scanned the room before walking to the barkeep. A large, bearded man with a clean apron greeted the party from behind the counter.

"Greetings, friends," he boomed. "I'm Ben. Welcome to the White Deer. What can I get you?" The rest of the patrons pretended not to stare, but their conversations quieted, and some risked casual looks to see who had entered. Chip noticed a black hooded figure in the far corner. He could not make out the face. A robust hearth on the other side of the room could not drive away the shadows under his cowl. Chip turned to avoid staring and thought he noticed the figure raise his head slightly.

"We are passing through on our way to Calgar," answered the wizard loudly. "We seek food and shelter for the night."

The barkeep shook his head. "It's all full tonight, I'm afraid, unless you count the barn. Many travellers are on the same mission as you. I have a pot of venison stew over the fire if it pleases you."

"It pleases us, and so does the barn. We would welcome a roof over our heads tonight." Xander smiled.

Ben looked like he was going to object then shrugged. "Suit yourself. I can give you a good rate. A little more if you want the fire on in the wood stove." He pulled five bowls out from under the counter and a loaf of fresh bread. "Help yourself to the stew. Ale?" They all nodded.

The barkeep left the room through the back door and reemerged a few moments later with five large tankards in his meaty hands. A young lad followed him out. Ben, the barkeep, set down the ale as they seated themselves with full bowls of steaming hot venison. Each tore off a piece of warm bread.

"My stable boy here will take care of the horses and light the fire in the barn. You can have one more helping of stew." The barkeep started to turn, then looked back and asked. "Any news from Vanalon?"

Chip noticed others at nearby tables leaning over to hear.

Xander nodded. "The soldiers defended Vanalon bravely and protected their queen. In the end, they defeated the first demon horde, though at great cost. The Calgar army is providing reinforcements to defend the city from the next attack. Be prepared to leave at a moment's notice when the soldiers begin retreating." Ben nodded grimly.

Another patron, two tables over, snickered and spoke in a voice that carried throughout the room. "Who says they will retreat? Even if this demon rabble exists, they can't stand up to the training of a thousand Calgar soldiers. There is no need to go anywhere. Besides, I have not spoken to a single person who's even seen these supposed demons."

"That's because they are all dead," Xander answered with a tepid smile and mirthless eyes. "Except for us and a few others, no one has seen a demon and lived."

The patron and a skinny man sitting with him looked at each other with blank faces, then laughed simultaneously. The one who spoke was a large man with burly arms. He slammed down his empty cup of ale and doubled over. The wizard calmly took another bite of stew. Garth Stone's implacable face did not change a single creased line as he stared at the villager as if studying an insect. The big man's skinny friend noticed the weapons master's look and let his laughter die off in a nervous giggle.

Ben turned to the patron and admonished him. "Settle down Borf. All these villagers are not fleeing for nothing. The Calgars would not send a thousand men to Vanalon to stretch their legs. This gentleman is simply providing news is all."

Borf chortled, "Ain't no such thing as demons. You go ahead and believe that after three thousand years, these creatures are running around the countryside eating people. The Calgars are only here to stop these fake rumours and kick out that weak, spineless King Rupert, who is just a fatter version of his dead father."

Both men let out loud laughs and slapped each other on the shoulders. Some other patrons joined in, nodding in agreement. Eleanor shot the men a murderous look, but Xander rested a hand on hers. The barkeep looked uncomfortable, shaking his head.

"Not only are there demons roaming the countryside," the wizard countered, interrupting the laughter, "but they take orders from Dark Elves who pay homage to the Unnamed One."

There was a brief silence, and then the two men laughed all over again. The other conversations in the room stopped as all eyes turned to hear the patron's response. "Dark elves?" Borf managed, gasping for air. "Nobody has seen an elf since the Great War. They probably aren't real either." He continued chuckling, holding his beer belly.

"Oh, they are real," Xander said loudly enough for everyone to hear. "There is one sitting over there." The wizard pointed at the hooded stranger alone in the corner." Borf looked over as the figure raised his head, and the laughter caught in his throat.

Two green eyes blazed to life within the shadows of the black cowl. Pale hands shot from the sleeves, sending out ropes of green magic streaking towards Xander, who calmly formed a blue shield. The green magic disappeared into the blue barrier, and the Dark Elf stood in fear before leaping for the window. The wizard extended a hand and froze the elf in midair. Xander's eyes crackled a fierce blue. He spun the Dark Elf around and levitated him towards the table. The hood fell off, revealing a cold, white face with almond-shaped black eyes and pointed ears.

Borf stood mortified as if one of his childhood nightmares had come to life. Wetness appeared around his crotch as the elf's face passed within inches of his own. Borf's friend fell back in his chair, pulling up his knees in fear. Cries of shock erupted from several other tables.

Xander's voice drowned them out. "Whence have you come, Dark Elf?" he intoned. The being hissed but did not respond. "Who sent you?"

The Dark Elf stopped struggling, then laughed evilly. His toes hung a foot off the floor. "We are coming for you and the boy, wizard." His laugh turned menacing. "You cannot escape us..."

"Who sent you?" he repeated.

"My Master sends us all, may we grovel at his leisure. He will find you... You cannot hide..." The elf grinned wickedly, eyes crackling bright green, as he grabbed his own black dagger and stabbed it upward under his chin. The point went hilt deep straight into his brain. He died with a frozen smile.

Xander opened his hand, and the dead elf fell in a lifeless heap. "Is that proof enough for you, Borf?" he asked, taking another bite of stew. The patron slumped into his chair in shock.

"I... I meant nothing by it, Mr. Wizard," he stammered. The rest of the room sat motionless. Nobody made a sound.

Xander glanced around the room. "Spread the word of what you saw here. The demons are real, and so are the Dark Elves. An evil greater than you can imagine is coming. Flee to Calgar and help bolster the defences of the city. Only by working together do we stand a chance against this monstrous foe."

The other villagers and travellers nodded solemnly.

"Yes, sir."

"Yes, Mr. Wizard."

"Will do."

Xander sat back and signalled to the stunned barkeep, who forced himself to walk over with shaking hands. "One more round of ale, and then we will retire to the barn for the evening. Do not disturb us, please. Here's for your trouble." The wizard dropped three silver pieces on the table, and Ben nodded wide-eyed.

"That is more than enough. Have as much stew as you like." The barkeep lowered his voice. "Thank you for that demonstration. It's high time everyone saw what was going on. The Dark Elf entered about an hour before you. He would not show me his face when ordering ale, and I did not pry. I assumed he preferred to be alone. I should have been more vigilant."

Xander sighed. "If you had, you would be dead. Take no blame, Ben. If you ever get questioned by a Dark Elf, answer truthfully, and you might live. I suggest you be ready to leave on a moment's notice if things get worse. Thank you for helping these travellers on their way." The barkeep bowed before lifting the dead Dark Elf over his shoulder, then exited through the back.

Xander finished his bowl of stew. Garth had already stood and was helping himself to another. Chase looked around, shrugged, and took his empty bowl to the fire for a refill. Chip leaned towards Eleanor, who still looked annoyed.

"Are you alright?" he whispered. She looked into his eyes, and the anger left.

"Yes. My brother and father had many faults but still had some good qualities. I feel obligated to defend my family."

"I understand. Some of these villagers are plain fools." Chip put his hand over hers.

She nodded sadly. "I have lost so much already. Please don't leave me."

Despite everything, the boy laughed gently. "Never. Besides, where would I go?" The response elicited a small smile from the princess, who squeezed his hand.

The companions ate their fill, and Xander stood up to usher them out. Ben came forward to escort them to the front door and gave directions to the barn. Some patrons bid them good night, while others thanked them.

The night air was cool and refreshing. They followed the wizard to a walkway around the inn that led to the barn. The stable boy stood at the open doors. Behind him, a fire roared in the wood stove along the wall.

"There are blankets and straw pillows in the loft," the stable boy said, standing straight. "I have filled several pitchers of water from the river. If you need anything else, knock on the inn's back door." The groom bowed low. He must have heard about the events in the tavern and gave them a parting look of wonder and curiosity. He had likely not met a wizard before.

Xander nodded. "Well done, lad. We will not need anything else this evening. Let us know if you see any strange people entering the inn tonight or in the morning." The boy stopped with a perplexed look, then nodded in understanding. Xander flipped him a silver coin, and the groom gave a little jump at his good fortune then bowed low and departed.

The barn floor was bare other than bits of straw. Half a dozen chairs sat in a circle around the wood stove. On an old oak table were several pitchers of water with earthenware cups. Various pitchforks and other tools hung on the walls. The smell of wood and hay was prominent.

The wizard looked at the rest of the party. "I did not intend to draw unwanted attention, but if it will save lives, so be it. We are still on the road to Calgar, so I am not too concerned. Others, however, could have sensed the use of my magic if they were in the vicinity. We must set up a watch tonight for two hours each. Who would like to take the first one?" Chip raised his hand. "Good. The rest of you should sleep. We still need to recuperate."

Chase yawned. "You do not have to ask me twice. Wake me for the second watch." He turned and climbed up the ladder to the loft.

Garth walked over to Xander. "Word will get back to the Dark Elves that an older magic wielder left Vanalon. They will likely assume it is you and know that the great wizard Xandrostika is not defending the city anymore. They may attack sooner."

Xander sighed. "I must admit I did not expect a Dark Elf to be sitting in the common room of the White Deer Inn. I still hope the three wizards from Calgar will fool them for a while after donning blue robes. It is unlikely the enemy knows how few Blue Levels remain at the Wizard's Guild. If so, we may indeed be in trouble." Xander sat down in front of the wood stove, pondering. "We could have camped beside the road, but I felt it was important to gauge the villagers' reactions to events. I hope our story will spread tonight and convince many to flee to safety."

The weapons master nodded.

"How did you know he was a Dark Elf?" Chip asked curiously.

"He did not sip his full beer once," Xander said, shrugging. "Elves hate ale. They only drink wine and he also looked the part. I did not truly know until I called him out. It looks like I guessed right."

Chip looked at him in wonder and shook his head. "Morgo could tell who a magic wielder was," the boy paused in reflection, "yet only when they were of age and had broken through their Wall." He remembered the general's surprise when Eleanor revealed her magic.

"Morgo had given up his humanity to be able to sense another's Power, even if they were not using it, which is unique," Xander remarked. "I do not believe there are others like him. Few would make that bargain. The rest of us cannot detect a magic wielder if their Wall is up. Even Dark Elves who have permanently removed their Walls cannot be sensed until they draw upon their Power. We can only sense another's magic if they use it or we link. A third possible way is to delve into their minds, as Elohan and Morgo tried with you. Somehow, you could stop them and, more importantly, see their memories." The wizard looked puzzled. "May I ask how you managed that?"

"Easy," said Chip, "I just wrap them in the Calm." Garth looked up and smiled.

Xander looked suspicious. "That is a training tool, is it not?"

The weapons master interceded. "Calmness is mastery. The Calm enables a person to relax and focus, eliminating mistakes based on emotion. It allows a fighter to react to the moment by letting habit take over. In many cases, if you think, you are dead. The Calm allows training to bypass risky emotions by achieving inner serenity. It is a level of mastery that few achieve. The boy's Calm may not be magical but is powerful nonetheless."

The wizard considered this. "Calmness is indeed mastery. When a magic wielder enters another mind uninvited to sense their Power, they usually expect fear or resistance. If a soothing Calm surrounds their presence, they likely do not recognize it or do not understand how to react. This gives Chip time to look into their memories. He seems to be able to go through a lifetime in moments. I am not sure a magic wielder has ever been so trained in using the Calm." He studied the boy. "Come and sit. I will enter your mind if you allow me. Try to surround me with the Calm."

Chip shrugged and sat opposite him. The princess moved beside them to watch. Xander's eyes blazed blue, and the orphan felt a presence enter his mind. The boy slipped into the Calm easily and wrapped the wizard in it. He felt Xander's mind calm down with him, relaxing it. A long array of memories appeared. Some were the ones he had shown the boy when he was much younger. Exotic places and people flashed before him, igniting a yearning in Chip to experience those adventures.

He saw Xander as a small child raised in a great fortress many times the size of Vanalon's palace. It jutted out on a monstrous cliff high in the mountains overlooking a vast plain. He next jumped to Xander and his brother Balor, standing beside a powerful-looking man with white hair. It could only be their father. Arkan sat at the head of an immense table surrounded by wizards and mages of many colours and races. Most wore blue or brown robes, while a few wore yellow and green. Many of these magic wielders were older with long white beards.

Huge troll mages covered in thick, bark-like skin sat beside dwarves with neatly trimmed beards. At the other end of the table was a contingent of Light Elves resplendent in long, flowing white robes. Their almond-shaped eyes were blue or brown, indicating their Level of Power. Most had long silver hair fastened with gold circlets revealing pointed ears. Wearing a shimmering crown, the Light Elf King sat at the end with piercing blue eyes.

"We must act, High Wizard Arkan. He has the Orb of Power. We must find a way to retrieve it," the Elf King spoke musically. All eyes turned to the head of the table.

Arkan spread his hands. "I know, King Luminor, but Morgo will sense any thief we send in. He will recognize our Powers, let alone our features."

"Not mine," Xander said. He looked to be about Chip's age in the memory. "He has never seen me. I can move quickly and take it before he knows."

Arkan turned. "You are brave and powerful, son. However, you are no match for Killian. Morgo will also be close by at all times."

"Then we set up a diversion in their camp," Xander insisted. "I know I can do it."

The High Wizard began to shake his head, and then a huge troll mage wearing a stone crown spoke up. "My magic can make him wear the guise of an Inner Circle member. With some help, I can craft the image to persist the entire night." The troll's voice was like the sound a large oak tree would make while walking.

Elf King Luminor nodded. "Thank you, King Jaggar. Xandrostika is young, but Morgo may not recognize his magic, at least initially. In addition to disguising him, we can surround the boy wizard with a barrier hiding his newfound Power. It should work as long as the general is drawn far enough away. With a proper distraction, we have a chance. We cannot survive this battle if Killian holds the orb. We are at the end of times."

Arkan sighed and finally nodded in agreement.

Chip then flashed to all the wizards, mages, and Light Elves lining up on the Desolate Plain linked to Arkan, who held the Orb of Power. They were erecting the barrier, which rose before them like a white curtain. All were straining to their utmost, including Xander and Balor, who stood beside their father. On the other side, they could sense Killian and the Inner Circle using all their Power to tear it down. The orb was too powerful, though, and the barrier grew to near completion.

When it looked like it would work, several Inner Circle members gave their spirit essences to tear it down. Arkan cried out, knowing that if it fell now, they would not be able to erect another in time and would be sitting ducks on the Desolate Plain, bereft of Power. Granted, he had the orb, but he would not have any Power left to magnify. The barrier began to buckle. Several wizards collapsed under the strain. They could not hold it much longer. Arkan turned sideways and looked at his boys with tears in his eyes.

"I am proud of you both," he said to them. His eyes then turned from blazing blue to bright white. He lifted the Orb of Power and channelled his spirit essence through the white stone into the barrier. When it struck, an explosion of light strengthened the shining wall, and it built to completion. The link vanished, and the orb fell to the floor of the Desolate Plain, now dark. Several other magic wielders collapsed in exhaustion. The Light Elves trembled from the effort. Arkan's blue robe sank to the earth, empty.

"No!" screamed Xander. Tears streamed down his face. Balor stood in shock.

King Luminor staggered over and picked up the now-dark orb. His eyes were wet as he looked at Xander. "Your father saved the world, son. Some day, we may need to do the same." He rested his hand on the boy's shoulder, then slowly walked away.

Chip flew forward to the Wizard's Guild. They were in the same room of the fortress as before, but now Balor sat in the seat of High Wizard. The great table was almost empty. A few human wizards and a single dwarf mage sat with worried expressions. All seemed nervous. The seats where the troll mages once sat were empty. The Light Elves were gone.

"The troll army is almost at our gates," a young, blue-robed wizard said urgently. We must abandon the fortress."

"The Guild has stood for a thousand years, Skylar," Balor said bitterly. Scarcely more than a boy, Xander sat to his left, looking defeated. "Where is everyone?" The High Wizard looked around at the empty seats.

Skylar stood. "I have foreseen this path in the prophecies. Powerful troll mages approach with a huge army from the north. Nobody has come to our aid. The High King of Toron has abandoned us. He says the Great Battle devastated his forces, and he refuses to spare his reserves. Our oldest members perished in the battle. The dwarf mages have defected, save one.

"As you know, other members left in protest when you took the seat without a vote. After you demanded its return, the Light Elves disappeared with the Orb of Power. We are all that remain. We cannot defend the Guild, High Wizard Balor. King Jaggar of the trolls is your equal in Power, and he has a significant number of mages.

Move south and rebuild a new Guild near Toron. This place is too close to the Troll Kingdom anyway. We must go now before it is too late. I beg you."

Xander looked up. "It's over, brother."

Balor looked at him in rage. "I say when it's over!" he screamed.

Chip shot forward again. He watched as Xander ran from the king of the Ancient City.

"Bring him to me!" the Red-Eyed King shouted in a terrible voice. Xander looked backwards and saw the tall being bearing down on him, holding a mighty sword. Chip felt a jolt of shock when he saw the Red-Eyed King. He seemed strangely familiar. His control over the Calm slipped. Xander pulled away and left his mind.

The wizard had a look of surprise on his face.

"I see now how you do it. Your control over the Calm is so complete that my thoughts are dispelled, including suspicion. When I am in your Calm, I have no thoughts. I even forget why I am there. I only have my memories. When you go through them, I get entranced as well. For the ones I consider private, there is a sense that someone is watching them, which perturbs me.

"After a while, a simmering anger that I am being invaded develops, and I can finally break free when I recognize what is happening. I figured it out while you were going through my memory of the broken Wizard's Guild after the Great Battle, but I allowed you to continue. I shot us to the Ancient City to show you the Red-Eyed King. I wanted to see your reaction, and it was, to say the least, interesting." He sat back, looking at the boy in an appraising way. "What did you feel when you saw him?"

Chip paused. "I..." The wizard leaned forward. "Ah, it's too crazy."

Xander rolled his eyes. "What is too crazy?" he asked, sounding mild.

The orphan squirmed. "I know it's impossible, but I felt for a moment that I recognized him." The wizard's eyes narrowed. The boy tried to elaborate. "He just... looked familiar. I also felt a feeling, an energy, or something. I'm not sure."

"Hmmm," the wizard looked cryptic, "I see." Xander sat frozen in thought for a moment, then slapped his thighs. "Well, off to bed then."

"Huh," Chip said, frustrated. "So what does it mean?"

"No idea." The old man stood up and stretched. "Will dwell on it. Good night." He climbed the ladder to the loft and disappeared over the top.

Garth gave the boy a wry smile and followed suit. Eleanor covered her face, trying not to laugh. Chip stood there bewildered, then finally raised his hands in defeat.

"Why me?" he said to no one in particular.

The princess grabbed his hand and pulled him down next to the warmth of the fire. He did not resist, suddenly realizing how tired he was. Chip stared at the dancing flames through the open door of the wood stove, contemplating. The wizard had lived an extraordinary life. Chip had viewed only a fraction of Xander's memories, but they were important ones. He wondered if the wizard showed them on purpose or if, by their very nature, were stronger than the others and surfaced.

"What did you see?" Eleanor asked, pulling her chair close.

He realized again how beautiful she was and lost himself in her eyes. Chip recounted the wizard's memories. "Xander showed me epic battles and historical events. I now realize his sacrifice and how important it is to fight the darkness. Countless people have given their lives for us to be here. I don't want their sacrifices to be in vain."

The princess nodded with a look of sadness. "I cannot believe my brother and father are gone." A tear slid down her cheek. He put his hand on her arm and bowed his head. "I will make sure their deaths mean something," she vowed. Chip looked up and saw fierce determination in her eyes. "I will not stop until every last demon and their foul king are gone from this Earth."

He stared at her and felt a sense of pride. "Your Power is very strong. I sensed it when we linked to heal the weapons master. It may even equal Xanders. Morgo said you are the strongest Brown he has ever sensed, and the general has been sensing others' magic for millennia. You can do much good with that kind of Power." She looked at him in surprise and wonder.

He looked at her askance. "What is it?"

She finally smiled. "You do not get it, do you?"

"Get what?"

She turned to face him. "I sensed your Power, too. It is… vast." She struggled to describe it. "Xander was only a fraction of your strength. Even though you had little left at the time, the space your Power holds is…" The princess held his face in her hands. "I believe you can save us all."

The orphan looked at her and finally began to believe in himself truly. He let go of the tremendous burden he had been carrying for so long. He had desperately tried to prove himself his whole life. As a young boy, Chip was ridiculed and scorned for being a lowly orphan. Miss Stern degraded and tormented him until his very spirit lost hope. It seemed by sheer luck that a few people took interest in him, and he clutched at that, trying his hardest to prove his worth to them.

He fought day after day, training and improving, promising never to give up. Yet even that did not seem enough. He could not save Farn and Sally, nor the two hundred soldiers defending Vanalon. Yet, he at least had enough to save Beth and Han from the dragon, enough to save the princess from Morgo, and enough to heal the weapons master. Perhaps he did have enough to save them all.

A sobering realization struck the boy. "Don't forget the Unnamed One has the red magic and has absorbed the Power of the white-eyed demons. His strength must be colossal." Chip shook his head, then abruptly shrugged and smiled. "Nothing a lowly orphan can't handle, right?"

The princess laughed. "We will find a way. We must. I believe in you." She turned, resting her head on his shoulder, and gazed into the fire. Chip felt a confidence build in him along with something else. Her determination and resolve gave him strength yet also simmering anger. This Demon King had tormented humans for far too long. He would find a way to stop him.

The orphan looked into the fire with her and lost himself in the dancing flames. Memories, some not his own, flashed through his mind with hopes, dreams, fears, and desires. He laid his cheek on the top of her head and vowed to protect her and all humankind.

The two-hour watch went by slowly. Within minutes of their talk, she had fallen asleep on his shoulder. He forced himself to stay awake, which was difficult as he listened to her rhythmic breathing, which sought to lull him into sleep's warm caress. He dared not disturb her, so for two hours, he did not move. It comforted him that she was resting. As the watch ended, Chip finally helped her to a sitting position. She woke and smiled.

"Rest now," the princess murmured, "I will take the next watch."

"No," he objected, "Chase is ..."

"I am not asking," she said, standing up and stretching.

"I will wait with you then," he said, trying to sound like Garth.

She laughed. "No, you will not. I am still a princess, am I not?" Before he could answer, she pulled him up. "I order you to bed." He tried to get another word in, but she pressed a finger to his lips. She continued to walk him over to the ladder leading up to the loft with her finger firmly in place. They both stifled a giggle. Finally, she had to let go as he began climbing the ladder.

"At least let me sleep down here with you!" he whispered. She shook her head.

"No, I want you to have a restful, uninterrupted sleep for the rest of the night." She held up a finger in warning, trying not to smile. "Now go."

He scrunched his face in mock anger, then sighed in resignation and climbed to the top. Chip let his vision adjust to the dark and found an empty cot with a blanket and straw. He debated removing some clothing, but the cool darkness enveloped him, so he settled down without resistance. The boy pictured the princess trying not to laugh while she pressed her finger on his lips and smiled. He wanted to hold the image longer, but darkness pushed in from all sides, and he fell into a deep sleep.

2

The orphan awoke to whispers below. Bright beams of sunlight slanted through cracks in the wooden barn like an ethereal white forest. Each ray highlighted the dust motes and bits of straw in the air, which smelled of hay and manure. Chip sat up, realizing he was the last one to awake, as usual. He felt refreshed and full of energy.

"The dead do rise!" Xander intoned from below. Chip wondered how the wizard knew he was awake when all he did was sit up without a sound. He shrugged and stood up, stretching languorously.

The smell of bacon and eggs wafted up to the loft. Chase opened the door and yelled to the stable boy to bring another breakfast. Within moments, Chip was downstairs, a heaping plate before him.

"It's midmorning," the wizard said, giving the boy a reproving look. The others tried not to smirk. "Lucky we went to bed early, or else we would be here until evening." Chip grinned despite having a full mouth. "But rest is important given the events of the past few days, so let's be off as soon as that plate is empty, shall we?" The orphan nodded. "Good, we need to reach the Great Plains the day after tomorrow. We are going to ...." He stopped, looking around as if the walls might have ears. "We will discuss it on the way."

The boy made short work of his meal, and they saddled up, preparing to leave. Ben, the barkeep, came out the back of the inn with his groom in tow and approached the wizard. "If more Dark Elves come and ask questions, what would you have me do?" he inquired.

Xander considered. "Tell them the truth. I do not want to put you in any danger. They have ways of finding out information if they think you are lying. Tell them we did not give you our names, but we are on the road to Calgar. Keep your ears open to news from Vanalon and prepare to leave when the city falls. Let the other villagers know this threat is real. It is not a question of 'if' the demons are coming, but 'when.' Thank you for your hospitality." He flipped the barkeep another silver coin and the stableboy a bronze.

"Thank you, kindly. May you find fortune in your travels," Ben said formally. The groom bowed low.

"Indeed, may we all find fortune in these dark days," the wizard said, giving them a courteous nod and kicking his horse's flanks. The others bade them well and followed.

The companions headed east on the One Road. Midmorning's bright sunlight shimmered through the autumn leaves. Great sloping mountains rose on either side of the valley like stern, immovable sentinels guiding them to the lands beyond. A cool wind travelled down the slopes as accompaniment.

They rode briskly for the rest of the day, only stopping for lunch. They passed other travellers who were on foot or horse-drawn carriages. Some had wagons full of most of their worldly possessions, pulled by old farm horses, while others wore backpacks and trudged down the road. All had the goal of reaching Calgar ahead of the demon hordes. Several travellers tried to make small talk or ask for news, but Xander kept details to a minimum. His main message was to continue to Calgar as the threat was real.

A few travellers recognized them from the recent tale of a wizard killing a Dark Elf in Deer Run earlier that day. Xander reported it was true and to heed the warning in the story. Nobody recognized Garth, who had donned a deep hood and spoke little. There was a possibility that a traveller might recognize the High Commander of Vanalon, so he remained hidden. Chip wore his usual red cloak, but he did not fear recognition. Those who had witnessed his feats were long gone or dead.

The small party rode until early evening, passing several more hamlets before arriving in the small village of Forest Glen. There was an old, quaint structure named 'The Oak Inn' at the far end of town. The wizard rode around to the back this time and knocked loudly on the rear door. The rest of them stayed close to the barn with hoods drawn.

The door opened, and a short, bearded man emerged. There was quiet talk and a flash of coins, and the wizard returned. Chip was hoping to stay in one of the rooms in the inn but understood the importance of keeping a low profile. He had never stayed in an inn before. Perhaps one day he would.

The barn was quite comfortable once they lit a fire in the metal stove. The barkeep's wife came out and stabled the horses, then rushed back to bring them hot stew and ale. The inn was likely too small to afford a groom to care for their mounts. The woman bowed and left, leaving the party to enjoy their meal on a rickety old table in the barn. Chase dug in immediately, then made a face.

Xander gave the tall boy an amused look. "Not to your liking?"

"It's rabbit. Not my favourite," Chase shrugged and continued eating.

The wizard clapped his hands together. "Ha, it is my favourite!" They all proceeded to eat heartily.

"I assume we do not want to draw attention to ourselves or meet another Dark Elf," Chip said to the wizard between bites.

"Correct. From this point forward, I prefer to be discreet. I hope the events in Deer Run convinced enough villagers to make it to Calgar sooner rather than later. My goal is to save lives. There is a risk that certain humans will provide information to our enemy, but it is unavoidable."

Eleanor raised her eyebrows. "No human would help those foul demons."

"I wish that were true," the wizard said, shaking his head. "There will always be people willing to sell anything for coin. Don't forget, it is unlikely a Dark Elf would reveal their identity to a human. Instead, they will remain hooded and offer coins for information. I'm afraid there is never a shortage of loose tongues. Soon, they will discover that a Blue magic wielder has left Vanalon in the company of others. They may already know." He paused, considering. "We need to check on something tomorrow, so go to sleep early tonight. I want to leave at dawn. I will take the first watch. Keep your eyes and ears open. Word spreads fast amongst villagers. Be vigilant." They all nodded.

The barkeep and his wife came to collect the empty bowls and mugs.

"Any more stew?" the woman asked with a homely smile.

"Yes, ma'am," Chase answered with a broad smile, holding out his empty bowl. The others laughed.

The wizard also raised his hand. "I will partake. It was delicious. We need one more round of ale, please and thank you. After that, we would like to retire early." The couple nodded and left. A short while passed, and they reappeared carrying a tray of food and drink.

"Before you leave, may I ask for news of travellers passing through?" asked the wizard.

The barkeep smoothed his apron. "More are leaving every day, sir."

"Any unusual travellers or events?"

"What do you mean?" the man answered.

"Oh, I meant, is there any news of strange tidings or cloaked figures wandering about up to no good." The wizard smiled.

The barkeep began to shake his head then stopped. His wife stepped forward with a look of concern. She began in a timid voice, "Figures have passed by recently in dark cloaks, hoods drawn." The barkeep shifted uncomfortably. "It started a few weeks ago. One came to the inn several days ago and stayed covered. He offered silver, but it was plain coins with no markings, which I thought was odd. He stayed one night in the rooms. We brought up food, and he opened the door with his hood still drawn. We did not think too much into it, but I felt something off late in the wee hours and decided to walk by the room. At the bottom of his door, I saw a glowing green light that terrified me. I returned to bed but stayed up the rest of the night."

"Can you sense magic?" the wizard asked.

Her husband shook his head. The woman stepped backwards, clearly uncomfortable. "I'm not sure what you mean."

Xander turned away so they could not see his eyes blaze blue. The woman shrieked and jumped.

"That answers my question." The wizard's eyes returned to normal. The woman looked scared, unsure what to say. The barkeep clenched his apron. "Stay your fears," Xander said soothingly. "I was checking if you could feel the Power. How long have you been able to sense?"

She looked at her husband, who shrugged in resignation. "Since I was a teenager. Nobody in the village knows." She looked fearful, "Some are superstitious."

"Quite alright." Xander smiled. "Your secret is safe with us. I also do not like revealing my gifts." He gave her a long look, and she nodded in understanding.

"Gifts should be kept secret," she said. Her husband murmured in agreement. The wizard provided another silver coin. "We would like to leave at dawn. Will breakfast be provided?"

"Of course," the woman said. "Expect it when the rooster crows." They bowed and hurried out.

The companions continued with small talk for another hour and then began to retire. The cots were again in the barn's loft.

Chip climbed in and closed his eyes. It felt like only a short time had passed before a hand gripped his shoulder.

"Wake up, sleepy head," Chase said. It took him a moment to realize where he was.

"What time is it?" the boy asked, rubbing his eyes.

"It's still two hours before the crow calls," Chase whispered. "I heard what I thought was a whisper outside recently, but when I peeked through the door crack, I saw nothing. It was probably just the wind, though there was an odd smell. Have fun!"

Chase clapped him on the shoulder, rolled over, and covered his head. Chip crawled out and slipped on his boots. He picked up his rolled cloak and then went backwards down the ladder. The boy stepped on the dirt floor and took a cursory look around. He approached the barn's doors and peered through the crack. Chip could see the inn, which had one light shining through the back window from an oil lamp. It was still pitch-black outside. He listened for a while but did not hear anything.

The boy walked over to the metal stove and opened it to examine the fire, which had died down to glowing embers. Feeling a slight chill, he added one extra log from the pile to the side. Two hours remained before dawn, and he wanted to maintain the warmth.

The orphan sat down and looked at the crackling flames through the open stove door. Now that he had been awake for a while, he felt better. Chip replayed the battle of Vanalon in his mind, wondering if he could have done anything differently for the two hundred soldiers who lost their lives defending the city. He hoped Han and Beth were safe with Auntie Clare on their way to Calgar. Though the boy had no love for Rupert, he still could not believe the king was dead, along with Biff, Chubs, and Gunter. Despite their qualities, they did not deserve to die. He shook his head and realized how close they had all come to dying in the throne room.

Chip thought of the man with the silver hair, who appeared in his spirit essence, and the incredible peace and tranquillity he exuded. The boy closed his eyes, remembering the feeling of peace.

A mournful howl sounded somewhere outside the barn. A memory stirred in the orphan's mind. He opened his eyes. Something was wrong.

The softest rustle sounded behind him. Chip whirled around to see a small, cloaked form climb over the top of the ladder and disappear into the darkness of the loft. He stood up to scream then felt a hot lancing pain in his left ankle, which sent him spinning around on his other leg. The boy cried out as he lost balance and fell backwards, landing on the stove. He shrieked and scrambled forward on his knees to come face to face with two assassin demons holding wicked black knives in their tiny fists.

At that moment, blue fire erupted from the loft, and a small flaming figure flew through the air, striking the opposite barn wall. Chip felt his back burn and frantically tried to pull off his cloak. The creatures leapt forward to impale him while his hands were occupied. The pain reached a crescendo, and even as they leapt, he blasted through his Wall, surrounding himself with a red shield of Power.

The knives of the assassins both hit their intended targets, which were his eyes and throat. The first knife went into his right eye hilt deep, and the other into his throat. The assassins laughed in delight, knowing they had taken out their Master's most desired enemy.

The small demons pulled their weapons back, only to look in shock at the smoking hilts of their now useless daggers. The blades had completely melted in the red envelope of Power surrounding the boy. Chip then stood up, eyes blazing a terrifying red. The assassins stepped back in distress, their wizened faces displaying fear. He extended both hands, lifting their small bodies in the air like pieces of straw.

At the same time, several larger demons burst through the barn doors and instantly charged across the dirt floor towards him. He flung the small bodies with horrific force at the oncoming demons. Their bodies burst into red flame and slammed into the creatures in front. The assassins exploded from the impact, pieces of them flying in all directions. More demons entered behind, including a giant spider creature. Two loud thuds to his right announced the arrival of Chase and the weapons master. They both stood with swords in hand, faces chiselled in stone. The demons poured through the open doors, spreading out in all directions. Xander stood with Eleanor in the loft at the top of the ladder. Both of their eyes blazed with magic.

Chip tried to walk forward, but his left foot screamed in pain. He stood back on his good leg and lifted his arms to unleash death. The boy's anger at being caught off guard translated into raging Power.

The huge spider creature ran up the side of the barn wall and leapt at him, but the orphan was ready. He halted the massive beast's body in mid-air with one raised hand, then filled it with red fire. Its eight legs wiggled in a frenzy as the bulbous body exploded in a shower of liquid flame, which rained down on the other demons behind.

The creatures had time to scream in pain before blue and brown blazing balls of fire ripped giant holes in their chests. Two managed to get through the firestorm only to have their heads removed by Chase and Garth. In moments, it was over.

Chip stood enveloped in red Power with fists clenched at his sides. He wanted to kill more demons, but none of them remained. "Release your Power," the wizard commanded. "Save it for another day."

The orphan looked at him with blazing red eyes then replaced his Wall. When the magic disappeared, Chip felt the searing pain in his ankle and let out a small cry. He scrambled for the Calm, immersing himself in its serenity and felt the pain subside to a dull throb. The wizard raised his hands and used his magic to put out the remaining spots of fire in the barn.

Xander and the princess climbed down the ladder to pull up a chair for the injured boy. Chip sat down slowly and winced at the pain in his back from the fire. The wizard examined his leg and watched as the boy's foot drooped down. The assassin's small dagger had severed the tendon at the back of his ankle. Chip clenched his teeth in pain. Xander held his hand out to Eleanor, who clasped it without speaking. They both closed their eyes, and he watched the Power flare behind their eyelids. A tingling went through his body, and then his back felt cool and itchy. His foot throbbed in pain as he felt his tendon pulled down and reconnected with the severed end. They continued pouring magic into the tendon until it strengthened. The skin melded together, and finally his foot felt whole again.

They both opened their eyes and brushed off the wave of pain and exhaustion that crossed their faces. Healing took a toll on the healer, but seeing the relief on his face made them both smile.

Xander stood. "That should do it. Your ankle will be sore for a few days, but you will be able to walk." He looked around at the dead demons. Black blood and demon parts littered the ground. He then turned to his companions. "Breakfast, anyone?"

Chase laughed. "Absolutely, I'm famished!"

The wizard rolled his eyes. "It was a joke. Chip, next time you take the watch, please turn your chair the other way?"

The boy blushed. "I'm so sorry. It won't happen again."

"Do not fret. Even I did not think they would be on us this soon. More demons have escaped the barrier than I anticipated. The Demon King is now focused on eliminating you above all else. We need to leave immediately. Dawn is around the corner."

They heard footsteps outside the open barn doors. Garth and Chase's swords appeared in their hands faster than thought.

"Excuse me. Is everything alright?" The barkeep and his wife materialized around the open door. They surveyed the scene of carnage, and the woman covered her mouth while he blanched.

The wizard walked over, trying to wave away the mess.

"Everything is fine. We had a little run-in with a few demons. Not a big deal." He looked around and grimaced at the mess. Reaching into the fat purse at his waist, Xander pulled out a shiny gold coin. The barkeep's eyes opened wide at the sight. "I hope this will help with the cleanup." He flicked the coin at the man who expertly caught it. "I am afraid we cannot stay for breakfast. We need to head straight for Calgar. Please have our horses ready."

"Right away, sir." The couple bowed and disappeared to complete the task.

Xander looked at his companions. "All magic wielders in the vicinity will sense the expenditure of magic we released and will draw to us like a moth to flame. Pack your belongings. We must leave now."

They all scurried to get ready. It felt awkward stepping over decapitated demon heads and dismembered spider legs to reach their belongings, but they managed to complete the task quickly. The stench of foul, dead bodies began to permeate the barn. They left the structure to find their horses saddled and ready. It was still night, but a glow of light on the horizon above the mountains to the east signalled the approach of dawn. They inhaled the fresh air in deep gulps.

The barkeep and his wife stood holding the reins for Xander. Their frozen smiles betrayed a desire to see this particular party on their way.

"Thank you kindly," the wizard said, mounting his horse. "Once again, we apologize for the mess. If anyone doubts the existence of demons at this point, let them know what you saw here. Leave two demon heads where those who still doubt can see they are real, perhaps on the side of the road outside town. You may wish to close your inn and head for Calgar soon. The demons are becoming more brazen and increasing in number. Good day."

The barkeep and his wife both nodded. "May the Creator shine on you."

"As on you." Xander urged his horse forward, and the party took to the One Road in the growing light. They rode briskly to distance themselves from the small village. "Keep your eyes open. There could be Dark Elves and demons in these woods."

As the morning progressed, the sun fully emerged in the blue sky. To the west, on the horizon behind them, ominous dark clouds were rolling in. The wizard glanced behind as the wind started to pick up.

"Something wicked is coming." His face grew grim, and he said no more.

They rode for most of the day, passing travellers and vacant homes. News of the events in the barn had not reached any ears yet, and they left it that way. Soon, the villagers would be talking. Chip hoped it would urge them to pack up and leave while they still could.

It was late afternoon when the wizard pulled up his horse. Some travellers were ahead on the road, so he waited for them to disappear over the rise. Chip noticed the mountains in the distance ahead were significantly diminishing in size.

"If we continue for a day's ride, we hit the plains and then one more day to Calgar. I intended to head north after reaching the plains to avoid the city. That is still my intention, but I need to confirm some suspicions first." He looked to his left, facing north. Two jagged peaks stood like menacing guardians. "This is Fang Pass." His voice grew somber. "It has been shunned for three millennia."

"Is this where the Unnamed One lived with the Dark Elves when they fled after the Breaking?" Chip asked, afraid to hear the answer.

"Yes," the wizard said softly. "A day's ride north of here is Cave Mountain. It was the home of the Demon King and his hordes. I need to see if my fears are realized. The trail leading up to the pass has recently been used." He pointed to a faint path ahead. "After the barrier was erected, we tried to enter the Unnamed One's empty caves, but he had sealed them with magic. The Light Elves carried the Orb of Power but journeyed their own way. My brother Balor wished to open the caves, but our magic was not strong enough. We left it as a tomb. Over the millennia, some wizards have tried, even through linking, to open them, but they have all failed. The Demon King used Red Level magic that none of us can penetrate to close the entrance. I wish to see if the caves remain sealed. If not, I fear someone with great magic has been released from the Inner Circle to unseal them. The bigger question is why the Demon King closed them off in the first place. What was so valuable in the caves that he wanted to keep hidden?"

The rest of the party looked at each other, mulling over what could lie within.

Chase looked like he was ready for another adventure. "I say we find out." He grinned. "Do we have to come back this way when finished?"

"No," the wizard answered. "From there, we can head due east to the plains. It is actually a shortcut. Be warned, it could be very dangerous. We must go through Fang Forest to avoid prying eyes from Cave Mountain. I have heard stories of those woods." He looked at them ominously. They noticed the dark clouds in the west moving closer. "We should go now. A storm is coming."

The companions set off from the One Road on the faint trail leading into the Fang Mountains. Chip shivered despite being warmly dressed, red cloak drawn tight. Most tales villagers wove to scare children into obedience originated from stories of these fabled mountains. The tales ranged from strange creatures wandering into their village in the dead of night to travellers entering the pass and not returning. No homes were located for leagues before or after the trail. Knowing this was the location of the Unnamed Ones's lair instilled a sense of caution in even the hardiest villager, whether they believed it or not.

The faint path led into a thick grove of pine trees, which blocked most of the sun. They only had a few hours left of daylight, so they moved briskly while still being vigilant. Any manner of creature or demon could lurk along this trail, which almost immediately began to veer upwards through the trees.

The two mountains on either side stealthily wedged them in, forcing the travellers to take the only viable route. The air started to cool as they wound higher. The sounds of the forest seemed a little strange, and a slow sense of dread began to overtake the small party.

"Keep watch at all times," the wizard whispered, eyes darting to the side. He took the lead, carefully allowing his horse to find proper footing. Roots and stones popped up as the path twisted and turned. They had to dismount and walk with the horses over particularly steep rises at several points.

The afternoon sun began to dip low in the west, almost hidden by dark clouds which had nearly reached them. As they went higher, the pine trees finally began to thin, and they could see the top of the pass.

Both mountains had now risen on either side of them, and they felt trapped between two huge fangs. The trail forced them into a single file as an icy wind sprang up, funnelling through the pass straight into their faces. On their right, the trail began to fall away into a deep crevice that got wider and deeper as they pushed on.

The path hugged the mountain on the left, decreasing alarmingly in width yet rising nonetheless. To their right was now a fall to certain death. They had to dismount and tightly hold their horse's reins, leading the nervous animals along the thin ledge. The wind strengthened, creating a shrill moan that pierced their ears.

Chip was not fond of heights and looked with chagrin ahead at the rising ledge that seemed to hug and follow the mountain's girth. He spared a look down to the right, which made him nauseated. The cleft had turned into a drop of several hundred feet straight down and only increased the farther up they went. The wind began to whip in a frenzy as the moan turned into a high-pitched whine.

The boy looked up to see dark clouds appear overhead. The light of the setting sun faded, and a strange alien dusk settled over everything. The one small redeeming feature was that the precipitous fall looked less clear as it became difficult to see the bottom. He looked behind him to see Princess Eleanor struggling behind Chase with a grim expression, trying to keep her head down. Their eyes met, and he put on a brave face to reassure her, but a sudden gust of wind buffeted him off the side of the mountain and then back to the edge of the ledge. Only the horse's reins, tightly gripped in his hands, prevented the boy from flying straight off.

He pulled himself back, this time hugging the wall on his left as much as possible. Chip's heart rate lurched until he could feel it pounding in his chest. He tried to find the Calm, but it was elusive. He forced himself to put one foot in front of the other, following the wizard ahead.

Xander turned and yelled something, but he could not hear it over the sound of the wind. They plodded forward, heads bent low against the screaming wind.

The party finally reached the crest of Fang Pass, the most treacherous part. Chip had been looking down at his feet, keeping close to the wall. The ledge had thinned even further until it was less than two feet wide. He risked one more look to the right and instantly regretted it. The drop looked to be a thousand feet straight down to black emptiness. The sun had disappeared, and a deep gloom permeated everything. The wind was at its apex, buffeting them mercilessly with wave after wave of frigid air. The sound had intensified into an unimaginable wail of unresolved grief. Chip shivered violently.

Straight ahead, the land dropped into a dark valley before rising again to the next set of peaks.

One mountain on the right was tall and bent, looking unnatural in the dying light. He thought he could make out small black holes dotting the western side about halfway up. It was immense but seemed to have no top, almost like a headless corpse. It still towered over the other mountains despite its lack of a normal peak. He knew without being told it was Cave Mountain.

Suddenly, Xander stopped in front of him, and he almost ran into his horse. The wizard turned around, hugging the wall. There was no sense in trying to talk above the screaming wind, so he pointed to a spot before him. Chip's eyes widened in horror as he followed the wizard's finger, which showed the path ahead had fallen away. For several feet, there was only air. Xander made a jumping motion with his hand.

Feeling ill, Chip watched as the old man calmly stepped back and leapt forward, landing on the thin ledge on the other side. The wizard wobbled for a moment then leaned against the wall, hugging it. In his left hand, he still held the reins of his horse. Xander stepped back to give the horse room and tugged on the animal's reins. At first, it resisted then leapt nimbly across. The wizard had to move fast to make room. He then waved the boy on, flashing a forced smile.

Chip rolled his eyes and walked to the edge in trepidation. The wind was so strong that it was getting difficult to move forward. The path ended in front of him. He looked down and felt his stomach lurch. The jagged rocks shone dimly a thousand feet below. To his right was all open air.

"Do not look. Just jump," Xander shouted. He could barely hear him. The howl of the wind seemed to reach a feverish pitch and then suddenly died off. For a moment, he looked around in disbelief. The wizard nodded in encouragement. The sky abruptly became much darker, and he saw thick, black clouds above him. Chip took a step back to jump.

As he did, an immense crack of thunder reverberated throughout the pass, followed by a jagged streak of lightning. It seemed to strike the top of the mountain above him. His horse leapt into the air in fear and landed wrong. One leg skittered off the ledge, and it scrambled to right itself.

Chip pulled hard on the reins towards the wall to help it regain balance. He could hear the others struggling with their mounts as well. As his steed found its footing, the skies opened, and torrents of rain fell in waves, drenching them.

As if rekindled, the wind sprang up again, throwing the rain sideways. Another clap of thunder rocked the small party. Chip felt trapped in a maelstrom of elements. Even his magic could not help him here. He searched for the Calm while hugging the wall. Xander was yelling at him, but he could not hear anything. A moment of abject terror overcame him, and he closed his eyes.

"Face your worst fears." The weapons master's voice cut through his thoughts. Whenever his fear became too great, he often heard those words in his mind. Chip searched for the Calm and then demanded it. He found it and immersed himself in its stillness. The boy opened his eyes and saw the chasm in front of him.

The wind pulled on his clothes, trying to tear him away from the cliff wall. Thunder and lightning played off each other, an interplay of light and darkness. He gripped the end of the reins in his left hand and looked up. Xander was on the other side, beckoning him forward. The path widened where the wizard stood, which gave him some comfort. The ground had become slick with rain, and he was unsure if he could make it. Yet, he had to. Taking a deep breath, the boy ran forward and leapt.

He landed on the other side, teetering for a moment, then stabilized himself. Chip hugged the wall and turned to urge his horse forward.

As the orphan tugged on his horse's reins, it reared its head sharply in protest, yanking him back over the chasm. He only had time to push with one foot and leap across. He managed to land back on the other side but crashed into his horse's chest. The animal stepped back too far, and its right leg slipped off the precipice.

For a moment, it looked like the horse would right itself, but its rear body was too far over, and this time, its whole hind end began to fall. Chip saw the reins wrapped tightly in his right hand as the horse began to fall off the ledge.

He unwound his hand desperately as the rear half of the horse pulled its front legs off too. The boy let go a little too late, and the momentum pulled him forward enough to make his toes slide over the edge. He windmilled his hands hysterically, staring down into the chasm below with empty air on all sides. Chip watched, as if in slow motion, as his horse fell off the ledge with its legs flailing in the air, dropping into the darkness below.

The Calm disappeared, and he knew total fear, certain he would follow the horse. His weight seemed too far forward, but luckily a gust of wind pushed him back enough, allowing his weight to center over the thin ledge. Then he felt a firm hand on his shoulder, and Chase was there pulling him back.

"Stop enjoying the view. Hurry up and jump," his tall friend yelled above the shriek of the wind. Chip could only look at him in amazement. The comment was so bizarre that it actually helped refocus his thoughts. He turned back to the chasm, facing his fears again, and leapt across a second time. This time, on purpose, he did not seek the Calm. Chip wanted to do it in complete fear to prove he could fight through it. He landed on the other side and hugged the wall until his terror subsided. The boy looked down to locate the remains of his horse but could not see anything in the gloom. A pang of sadness hit him at the plight of the poor animal. He moved several feet along to give Chase room to jump.

His best friend had zero fear of heights and leapt across without hesitation. Chase pulled on his horse roughly, and it jumped across to join him. Eleanor's face was white, but she clenched her teeth in resolve and looked dead ahead as she leapt. She landed perfectly, then turned back. The princess was an expert with horses, riding them regularly as part of her upbringing. She used both hands to tug the reins, and her animal leapt across gracefully. They all had to move further down the ledge to give the weapons master room to land.

Garth completed the jump without hesitation, likely the only one with no fear. Chip felt embarrassed for having so much difficulty and resolved to challenge his fears more aggressively in the future.

They continued down the path against the punishing wind and rain until it widened, and the elements began to lessen. The trail's slope changed to a gradual descent, and finally, the wind died down. The rain became a regular downpour. The chasm on their right grew shallower until they reached the bottom, whereupon it merged with the path.

"Wait here," Garth said and disappeared into the near blackness of the aperture.

"I have to say I do not remember it being that treacherous," the wizard muttered. "Three millennia ago, it was a wide ledge where four of us could walk side by side. Time does do its work, indeed. Even so, I feel fell forces were at work to make it difficult for us. The storm seemed unnatural. This place reeks of evil." He looked to the north at the dark hulk of the huge mountain ahead of them. "Behold Cave Mountain. That is where the Demon King raised his abominations. It is still a day's walk to get to the base. We must reach the forest cover in the valley ahead and then camp. We will arrive near the caves late tomorrow afternoon if all goes well. It is best to approach in the dark, making it difficult for possible sentries to see us. That is assuming anything is even there. I did not cross the pass in broad daylight on purpose. In this gloom, we should be safe from prying eyes."

Garth reappeared out of the darkness with Chip's backpack. "Your side bag was shredded, but your main pack seems intact. I cannot, however, vouch for the condition of the items inside."

"Thank you. The horse..." Chip said dejectedly.

Garth looked at him, and his face softened. "He died instantly." Chip nodded and sighed. The weapons master handed him his bag. "I know your fear of heights. You handled it well, considering you had to make that leap three times. We could have lost more than a horse there. Do not dwell on it. Ride with Eleanor as she is the lightest. Is that acceptable, Princess?"

Eleanor smiled and nodded. "He does not look that heavy. I think we can manage." She turned to Chip with an amused expression. He could not help but smile. The boy tied his saddlebag to her horse and climbed behind her. The wizard momentarily looked at the two of them then turned with a faint smile and led them towards Fang Forest.

3

It took them another hour to cross the rocky slope to reach the trees. By the time they arrived, it was completely dark. Stars should have blanketed the sky, but the clouds had stubbornly moved in, not budging. The air felt charged and heavy. A sense of dread seemed to permeate the entire valley.

The immense presence of Cave Mountain watched over them, waiting like a hulking ogre to snatch them up and never let go. Of course, ogres were only in stories, weren't they? Chip would ask Xander one day. For now, he remained focused on the dark mass of trees ahead of him.

They entered the forest but stayed near the edge, unfamiliar with the woods, and not wanting to venture too far in the dark. The wizard decided to make camp. The rain continued to come down, but the treed canopy lessened its effect. They were still cold and wet, yearning for a fire, but they all knew it was too risky. The companions set up their tents, crawled inside, and changed into dry outfits. It was challenging to talk outside due to the incessant rain, so they ate a cold dinner inside and prepared their bedrolls for sleep. Chip shared his tent with Chase while Garth bunked with Xander. The princess had her own.

Chase crawled under his blankets. "Why were you so scared to make the ledge jump? It was so easy," he whispered. Xander had asked them to make no loud noises to avoid unwanted attention.

Chip gave him a withering look. He had already tucked himself in, feeling blissfully warm and dry. "You know I'm scared of heights, and it was not that easy. Even my horse was terrified."

He could hear Chase try to restrain his laughter. "The weapons master is right. Do what you are afraid of over and over until you master it, and you won't be afraid anymore. Remember when you were scared to swim in the Rocky River outside of town?"

"What about it?"

"Within a week, you were begging to do backflips off the rocks."

Chip remained calm. "Yes, I remember. But the rocks were only five feet above the water line, and the river in that area was completely safe to swim in. I do not see how that compares to being stranded on the top of a mountain pass, looking down a gaping hole that you are supposed to jump over with a thousand-foot drop to certain death, on a slippery ledge barely wide enough to stand on, all the while being pelted by an insane lightning storm and a crazy wind intent on pulling you off the cliff, which you are clinging to for dear life, and then to boot, you have to make your horse jump too." He took in a deep breath.

"What's the difference?" Chase asked. Chip turned and punched him in the arm. "Ow." They both tried to stifle their laughs.

"Alright, I guess I see your point," Chase conceded.

"Wait until we trigger one of your fears," Chip said innocently.

"Like what? I don't have any...." Chase responded, trailing off.

"Haha. Spiders. Lots of them. Crawling all over you," Chip laughed gleefully. "I can't wait!"

"That's not fair!" Chase sputtered. "That is a fear everyone should have. It is as scary as anything. Who likes spiders?" Chip could hear him shiver in disgust.

"I hear caves have spiders."

Chase did not respond and returned the punch instead.

"Ow." They laughed again then decided to rest. Garth had taken the first watch. They would all take turns throughout the night. After such a harrowing day, the boys did not take long to succumb to a warm, deep slumber.

Nothing eventful happened overnight, and they woke as the first rays of dawn entered the valley. The clouds were still there and, if anything, looked more ominous than before. It was as if they were filling themselves up to bursting before releasing their full fury. The companions ate a light breakfast of leftover cheese and cured meat and then packed up. The ground was still wet from the rain the night before, and a rumbling sounded in the distance.

"Always stay in the cover of the forest," Xander intoned. "The trees thin out when we reach the base of Cave Mountain later this afternoon, but first they grow much larger and older as we travel deeper. There are many stories of what lies in these ancient woods. Most were created to scare children, but others are likely true. The problem is you never hear the stories from the ones who did not make it. They would likely be more terrifying than all the others. Keep your wits about you. Even if there are no demons present, there are things that reside in these woods that even I have no knowledge of."

They looked at each other with apprehension but said nothing. Garth was impassive as ever. Chase prodded Chip in the back, trying to get a reaction out of him, but he ignored his friend. The princess nodded, taking it all in stride. Chip marvelled at her strength. Many people thought a princess would be a spoiled, weak brat, but Queen Charlotte ensured Eleanor grew up with normal children. She wanted her daughter to experience the difficulties and challenges of life like others. The girl could certainly play the princess role if desired, but usually, she was content to be one of them. He admired her calmness and adaptability.

They all mounted their horses and continued deeper into the woods. Chip sat behind the princess again and thought she must wash with scented soap, as she always smelled like flowers. He enjoyed being close to her and felt he could better protect her when she was near.

They crossed faint game trails with strange footprints, but nothing was recent. The wizard seemed to be creating his own path. As they went deeper, the shrubbery and grass died out, and the trees grew, interlocking their branches to create a permanent twilight that carried whispers of ancient secrets.

A sense of dread permeated the air, and the sounds lessened until an eerie quiet surrounded them. The soft brown earth of the forest floor even masked the sounds of the horses.

Xander abruptly pulled up his mount, causing the others to stop.

"Something is watching us," the wizard murmured. A dead silence surrounded them. "Keep alert. We must try to avoid using our Power unless absolutely necessary. It would alert any magic wielder in the caves ahead. This silence is unnatural. Some things on Earth predate the Great Forget or were created from its after-effects, like Morgo. Even the wizards of old avoided this forest and took the long way around to the caves. Be mindful."

Everyone looked around nervously except Garth. Xander motioned for him to take the lead with Chase next. They would have the best chance to react to any physical threats first.

Chip reached down to make sure his sword was loose in its scabbard. Sometimes, he preferred the sword across his back instead of at his waist. It all depended on the circumstances.

He vowed to withhold using his magic until they reached the caves. Otherwise, this would all be for nought. They moved forward through the gloom. Chip's heart lurched as a white figure appeared to the side of a huge, ancient tree. Several more moved out from other trees surrounding them.

They looked like white wraiths come from the dead to take away their spirit essences, but he soon realized it was simply an uncanny fog created by the moist conditions. His mind was playing tricks on him. As they rode further, the fog intensified, and everything became discoloured by a hazy, white gloom.

The trees grew even larger with trunks they could not reach around even if everyone clasped their hands together and stretched to form a circle. The silence became deafening, and the impending sense of dread was unmistakable.

Suddenly, a deep booming sound reverberated throughout the forest, making the horses leap erratically. Only through years of riding experience were they able to stop them from bolting. It was an immense crash of thunder directly above them, signalling another storm. They all looked up into the gloom as lightning exploded in the clouds overhead, briefly illuminating the treetops far above.

Eleanor screamed first, and the others recoiled in shock as the short illumination revealed a group of enormous spiders hanging from their webs only a dozen feet above them. The eight-legged creatures dropped heavily, landing on the soft forest floor around them. They were brown and hairy, unlike the demon spiders, which were black or dark grey. These were slightly smaller than Chip and displayed menacing, wizened faces with large, intelligent yellow eyes. Long, curved fangs dripped a gooey substance that steamed when it hit the ground.

The mounts panicked and ran in all directions. The flailing horses' hooves crushed several spiders as they charged. One spider received a kick from Garth's steed and struck a tree trunk, exploding in a shower of green goo. Eleanor's horse bolted straight ahead, trampling a large spider directly in its path.

They plunged through the gloom, watching in horror as more spiders appeared ahead, dropping to the ground with fangs bared. Chip looked back to see the other horses darting around the creatures and fanning out in different directions. He pulled his sword out and hung on as the horse veered back and forth to avoid the terrifying creatures. One tried to jump sideways at him, but the boy was able to slice down through its face, causing green blood to spray onto the forest floor before it died. Another leapt from the other side, but he fended it off by swinging his sword around and severing its forelegs. It snapped at him with its long fangs, then fell awkwardly on its remaining legs.

The horse whinnied and continued running until no further

spiders dropped from the trees. Chip looked back with wide eyes as the creatures skittered across the ground, chasing after them.

As if reaching an invisible line, they slowed to a stop and then retreated. It was as if they had a boundary to their domain. He could not imagine what would have happened if they were on foot. The horse sensed the spiders were gone and slowed to a trot. The fog closed behind them.

Finally, they slowed their mount to a walk to let it rest. The sounds of the forest began to resume, signalling they were out of danger. Chip momentarily wondered what was ahead if giant human-eating spiders wouldn't go further.

The boy then remembered Chase's fear of spiders and wanted to laugh out loud, but the gravity of the situation got the better of him. He also realized his friend had no magic protection if he was in danger.

"Let's circle back, but don't get too close," Chip whispered in her ear. "We need to find the others and offer help if they need it."

She nodded and turned the horse left into the trees, doubling back in a wide circle. It did not take them long to find Xander approaching them from the opposite direction. He looked in good shape and pulled his mount up to theirs.

"Glad to see you made it. That was a nasty surprise." The wizard glanced up again, scanning the trees. The fog seemed to be lifting a bit, allowing them to see higher into the canopy. They felt relief to find no more spiders. The sound of thunder struck again, this time further ahead of them. No rain had fallen yet. "Let's go the other way and find Garth and Chase. I noticed their horses went right when they panicked."

The trio turned and trotted in the other direction, their eyes wary. A short time later, they heard other horses and saw the weapons master and Chase together. They still held on to their swords, which were dripping green spider blood. Chase had a disgusted, sickened look on his face, but it turned to relief when he saw them. Garth proffered a rare smile.

"Of all things, spiders! Why spiders?" Chase lamented.

"You weren't afraid, were you?" Chip said, trying to keep his face blank. Chase glowered at him.

"Be happy we were not on foot," Garth said, "We would have been swarmed. I suspect many travellers unlucky enough to wander through their nesting grounds have met untimely ends."

"Indeed," added the wizard. "Let's continue moving on. It is nearing midday, and we still have not reached the halfway point of this dreadful place."

They turned and continued north, Garth once more taking the lead. Chase's eyes darted back and forth, looking everywhere for more spiders, but none materialized. Chip tried not to laugh, picturing his big friend afraid of such a small creature. Then again, these were not small spiders by any means.

The rumble of thunder accompanied them, followed by a flare of lightning. The fog began to return, and the ground descended, becoming spongy. The air took on a fetid scent of decay and death. The light seemed to dwindle as it receded above them. The great trees shrunk, becoming bent and deformed before finally thinning out. The fog increased to a thick, opaque blanket that covered everything. Their descent finally levelled off, and then there were no more trees.

The ground became very moist, and patches of moss dominated. The stench of rot was thick. The forest sounds once again disappeared. This time, everyone felt a palpable dread as the fog rolled in from all directions. They pushed forward slowly, squinting ahead, covering their nose.

Garth's horse stumbled first, and they heard wet, suction sounds. The fog cleared enough to show the poor beast's front hooves were mired in the beginnings of a black, still lake. The water rippled outward from the animal's legs into the fog in ever-increasing ripples. The weapons master pulled up on the reins, urging his horse back. Instead, its legs sank deeper into the mud until the water reached its knees.

A loud rumble of thunder erupted, and a spider web of lightning lit up the fog around them. For a moment, they could see that the lake was quite large, extending outwards with no end in sight. Chip thought he could see dark shapes swimming towards them in the gloom, but the darkness returned.

"I thought I saw things in the water," he warned.

"I saw them too. They are swimming this way," Eleanor said with a rising note of fear.

Garth pulled hard on the reins, and the horse strained, trying to pull out its front legs. Finally, with a squelching sound, the hoof released, and its left leg began to pull out. As the hoof broke the water's surface, a green hand reached out of the black lake and wrapped itself around the horse's bent leg. The stallion screamed in terror.

Several more green hands appeared and grabbed the distraught animal, pulling it forward. Round green heads materialized out of the water, revealing evil-looking frog-like creatures with red eyes. Several more swam close until they crowded around the horse, grasping it with wet, slimy hands. Garth drew his sword and slashed down on both sides of the animal, but more green hands appeared, pulling the horse deeper into the water. The horse whinnied shrilly in panic. The weapons master lopped off more hands, but others replaced them.

"Get out of there," yelled the wizard. The horse stumbled, and its head went underwater. The weapons master fell forward, and slimy hands grabbed his legs. He lifted his feet out of the stirrups and stood on the saddle just above the water, then slashed in a circle around him. Garth lopped off green arms, but more appeared. The horse fell in deeper. The weapons master ran down the back of his disappearing mount as it became almost fully submerged and leapt off its hind end to land on the shore. The horse vanished under the black water.

Dozens of gleaming red eyes appeared above the water line.

"Back up," shouted Xander as the frog-like creatures began jumping out of the water straight at them. On land, the weapons master was in his element. His sword became a blur in the murky light as he chopped off heads and arms like a windmill. The creatures were eerily similar to frogs but grew to the waist height of a man.

Their mouths contained multiple rows of sharp teeth meant for snagging and tearing prey. The companions retreated as more creatures spilled out of the black lake.

Chase threw his reins to Xander, leaping down to assist Garth. Chip followed suit. The master and apprentices performed the dance of death until the bodies in front of them became piles. They continued to retreat to firmer ground, and the fog thinned. Then, as suddenly as they appeared, the multitude of creatures croaked at them and slunk back towards the lake. Plops sounded as they leapt back into the black water and disappeared. The three of them stood panting, swords covered in green slime.

"I see why there's a few tales about this place," Chase mentioned to no one in particular.

"Yes," Xander agreed, "its denizens are rather unwelcoming. This lake is well hidden, even from the slopes. I am not sure if the fog ever leaves it. Let us give it a wide berth and go around. Garth, I am sorry about your horse."

"It was a fine steed," the weapons master said stoically. "I will lead the way and walk for now. I can react better on my feet."

They nodded and followed him. The lake was not as wide as they thought, but nonetheless, they kept their distance. The fetid smell disappeared as they circled to the side, and a slight wind picked up, bringing cleaner air. Though it was past midday, they decided not to eat as smells might attract unwanted attention.

Garth continued moving steadily, not wanting to dwell in the woods longer than necessary. The ground began to rise again, and the giant trees returned. The hulking form of Cave Mountain appeared through slight openings in the canopy above, much larger than before. Dark, roiling clouds seemed to brood over the mountain, awaiting their arrival. The wind picked up, and the sounds of thunder increased in volume. They were heading towards the storm.

Mid-afternoon arrived, and the small party started to feel hope that the forest would end when the sounds around them suddenly died out. They looked up in fear, expecting to see giant spiders with long fangs hanging above them, but the canopy was clear. The fog had lifted due to the increasing wind speed, allowing them to see further, yet the gathering storm caused the light to fade. Nothing moved in the gloom. The weapons master instinctively pulled out his sword, and the others followed suit.

The companions crept forward, scanning the immense trees in the twilight. Ahead of them, between the massive trunks, was a clearing. They tied the horses to a cluster of small saplings trying to grow amidst its huge brethren and approached with caution. Chip looked around a giant bole before him and gasped.

The largest tree of all stood in the clearing ahead, an ancient behemoth easily sixty feet around. Strange markings surrounded the trunk, and a feeling of dread permeated the air, falling on them like a shroud. The monstrous tree commanded a wide berth as if forcing the others to grant it unimpeded access to the sun and rain. A ring of faded smooth stones surrounded the behemoth. A large, ancient-looking rectangular stone table sat on the forest floor before the tree. The stone appeared weathered over eons of time yet still held its essential shape. The top was heavily stained with a red substance that looked like blood.

Xander stepped into the clearing with a look of horror.

"Great evil was done here. The very earth is stained with the blood of the innocent. Dark rites have been performed here for millennia." He peered closer at the large rectangular stone table in front of the massive trunk. "Most of this blood is old, but some is quite fresh." He looked at the symbols on the tree and made a sign of warding. "Fell magic of the blackest kind is inscribed here. The Demon King made many sacrifices on this spot, human and demon alike, appeasing whatever force fed him. No animal of the forest will enter this clearing. We must not tarry long, for the Divide between the Light and Darkness is thin here. Make sure you do not touch this tree, for it..."

A sudden scream pierced the silence of the forest. They all tensed in fear, swords ready. A shout followed, then a shriek. Loud footsteps approached from behind the evil tree.

"Back," urged the wizard. They scurried to the edge of the

clearing and hid behind the trees surrounding it. The companions managed to conceal themselves as a party of demons entered the clearing to stand before the huge tree. Leading them was a lone Dark Elf wearing a long green cloak. A look of malevolent amusement covered his features. Five frightened humans were behind him, encircled by a dozen demons of various forms. Chip was having trouble deciphering the features of the people through the gloom, but he could make out three adults and two small children. The foul demons were trying to sacrifice an entire family. The boy's temperature began to rise in anger.

The Dark Elf turned around to stand behind the stone table, which Chip now realized was an altar. "Bring them forward, my pets," he purred in a voice dripping with anticipation, "I long to smell human blood. When it is over, you may feast on the remains."

The demons surrounding the terrified humans started mewling in joy as saliva dripped from their open mouths. They were an assortment of shapes and sizes, each more deranged than the last. One even resembled a scorpion, its long, black tail coming to a thin point. Several demons and the Dark Elf blocked Chip's view of the humans. He began to rise to put an end to this horror when Xander, crouched beside him, lifted his hand in a staying gesture. The boy nodded and waited.

The Dark Elf's eyes blazed green, and a crackling energy filled the air. He lifted his hands, pointing them at the giant tree. Nothing happened at first, but then the symbols and runes covering the bark began to glow a bright green.

At the same time, otherworldly sounds seemed to come from the tree itself. At first, it was distant cries and wails, which increased in intensity until ear-splitting shrieks enveloped the clearing. The cacophony of otherworldly voices built up to a terrifying crescendo.

At the peak of sound, with the Dark Elf straining from the effort, a black hand appeared in the middle of the runes to emerge from the tree itself. Chip's blood ran cold. A skeletal, metallic arm followed the hand, and then a grotesque head pushed itself out of the trunk. The face looked like a skull with black hollows for eyes that sucked the light out of the air. The mouth was a wide-open black circle with no teeth. Its skin looked to be of a hard metal-like substance. Something about the creature made it more fearsome than anything the boy had ever experienced.

Even the Dark Elf looked fearful. "Quick, we must feed it, lest it take us for its prey. Bring the weak humans forward." The circle opened, and the demons roughly pushed the captives into the eerie green light.

Chip could finally see the people. He almost cried out and rose to move forward as the light revealed Auntie Clare. She was with two male Vanalon soldiers and two children, Han and Beth. The Dark Elf must have captured them on their way to Calgar. The Wall appeared in his mind, and his rage rushed towards it. Then, Xander's presence was there, obscuring the Wall. The wizard also grabbed the boy's arm as he rose.

"No magic, wait," the old man whispered. Chip shook his head and pushed forward.

"There is a better way," the wizard insisted. Chip could not tell if Xander was speaking in his ear or his mind, such was his rage. "If you want to save them, stop." It took all the control the boy could muster to leave his Wall intact. He shook from the effort then nodded and crouched down beside the wizard.

The Dark Elf looked at the human captives. "Leave the boy, for he is special. Our Master will reward us greatly for him. He can watch his family and friends die. Give the little girl first as a taste and then the larger ones."

Xander waved to the weapons master, who nodded from behind another tree and reached for the long dagger in his boot. The demons picked up little Beth and brought her to the table, trying to hold her wriggling form flat. She screamed in her tiny voice, which caused the Dark Elf to laugh evilly.

The thing coming out of the tree was almost fully revealed. Its body was long and thin, as were the elongated arms. It paused to look at the little girl on the table, then opened its black mouth to moan. The sound was neither human nor demon but of something that signalled the death of everything. It spoke of emptiness, darkness, and the complete absence of existence. Even the demons holding the girl shrank back in terror.

Xander signalled, and in one fluid motion, the weapons master threw his dagger straight at the Dark Elf's back. As Garth revealed himself to throw the blade, the creature crawling out of the tree looked up, which was enough of a warning for the Dark Elf to react. He immediately surrounded himself with green magic. The dagger evaporated in the green fire, causing no damage. The elf released the shield and chuckled grotesquely as he turned to face them.

At that instant, Auntie Clare violently broke free of her demon captor and shot a tiny, concentrated ball of yellow fire straight through the back of the Dark Elf's head. There was a momentary pause of shock on the elf's face as it came out his eye, and then he fell to the ground dead. The creature climbing out of the tree uttered a dreadful sound then vanished back into the bark. The glowing green symbols and runes went dark. The rest of the companions leapt out from behind the trees and charged the surprised demons. They abandoned their captives to face this new threat.

Han darted across the ground, pulled his tiny sister off the table, and stood in front of her protectively. Chip ran out ahead of the others, fueled by a bloodthirsty rage. The first demon fell before him as the boy twirled, savagely beheading it mid-snarl.

Garth and Chase flew into the melee, becoming dealers of death. A small but agile spider demon managed to leap over the others and land on Xander, who calmly raised his sword, skewering it with its own weight. The two human soldiers pulled Auntie Clare away from the demons and then circled to gather the children. Han read the situation and was already urging Beth towards them, a look of defiance on his little face. Auntie Clare deftly picked them up and ran to the edge of the clearing.

The scorpion demon scurried crab-like at Chip, who turned to face it head-on. It had claw-like hands similar to a lobster and used them as pincers. He sprang back while making a vicious downward swipe of his sword, lopping off its left claw. The demon hissed, then whipped its tail forward over its body, trying to impale him with the tip. The boy swung instinctively, chopping off the end.

A fountain of black blood sprayed outward onto the ground. The creature shrieked and swung at him with its remaining pincer even as he brought his sword back. Chip was overzealous and blocked the claw with his forearm instead of the blade, causing the weapon to fly out of his hands. Immediately, he leapt back and drew both daggers from his hips. Though the sword was his mainstay, he was versatile and trained with many weapons.

The scorpion demon assessed the daggers with another hiss then leapt in aggressively. Chip used both weapons to block its pincer, flipped his right dagger, and drove the blade hilt deep into its eye. The demon pulled back, shrieking in pain, allowing him to dive for his sword. The boy rolled to his feet with sword in hand in time to counter the wind-milling claws of another demon with long fangs.

The scorpion thrashed violently in its death throes, knocking over several other demons before finally succumbing to its injuries. Chip barely had time to register this as he parried a flurry of blows from his new attacker before slicing the slender demon's arms at the elbows. From there, he slit it from crotch to throat, watching as everything fell out at once. He turned around to face the next attacker, but none were left. Garth and Chase were already cleaning their swords on the bodies before them and sheathed as one. They took a moment to eye each other's work then nodded with mutual respect.

Xander stood breathing heavily, his sword dripping with black blood. Everyone had refrained from using magic, except the small amount used by Auntie Clare. Chip looked around and spotted her and the children at the edge of the clearing. He hurried over, smiling with relief.

"Are you all alright?"

The others joined him. Han grinned and nodded. Beth still had tears in her eyes, so her older brother put his arm around the girl's tiny shoulders, which reassured her.

Auntie Clare stepped forward. "Thank you, Xander. I am not sure what we would have done without you. I do not have much Power, but I saved all my magic for that moment and released everything I had at the Dark Elf while he was distracted." The fact that she was a magic wielder surprised Chip. Then again, he was surprised by a lot these days.

She continued, "They ambushed us yesterday in the early morning on the One Road near the entrance to Fang Pass. The Dark Elf subdued us with his Power then had the demons guard us. We had no chance to escape. They marched us with no rest over the pass and across the valley into Cave Mountain last night. It was dreadful. There are other human captives in the caves. When the demons get hungry, they pull one of us out to eat." She looked at Han with sympathy. "One brutish creature announced he wanted a snack and picked up Han, dragging him to the front. There was nothing we could do. Somehow, the boy remained calm and unafraid. I was about to release my Power to stop it, knowing I would likely die, but before I could, a Dark Elf walked up and stopped the demon from eating the boy. He ordered it to release the child so he could inspect him. The Dark Elf knelt before Han and put his hands on the sides of the child's head. Nothing happened, and then he suddenly jumped up and ran to bring another Dark Elf with a shiny blue cloak."

"That sounds like Zoran," Xander said grimly.

Auntie Claire reflected, "Yes, the Dark Elf called him Master Zoran. The brutish demon thought it was all right to try and nibble Han's fingers off before they came back, but Zoran's eyes shone bright blue, and he destroyed the creature with his fire. He then walked over and put his hands on Han's temples. Zoran screamed and fell backwards. He looked scared and announced that he needed to examine all humans in the future before they were consumed. He ordered them to keep Han alive, as he was precious to his Master. Zoran then walked away, and we were finally left alone for the night, but they started eating more captives this morning. This continued throughout the day, and a while ago they brought us here to be sacrificed."

She recoiled, still recovering from her ordeal.

Auntie Clare turned to Chip and hugged him. "I am so happy you are alright. You have been through so much, my dear boy. I always knew you were special. I only have a little Power at the Yellow Level, but I help when possible." She held his face in her hands and smiled at him.

Chip looked into her eyes and felt a flood of emotions. He remembered her reading to him while he sat happily in her lap as a little boy. He had felt so safe and loved. A pang of guilt struck him for not visiting her more often.

"Han and Beth could not be in better hands," he said thickly. "Please take care of them. I am so happy you are safe."

She hugged him again, then brought the two children forward.

Chip kneeled and held their hands. "Are you alright?" he asked.

Han looked at him solemnly. "Beth was scared, but I knew you would save us." Chip gave him a perplexed look.

"How could you know that?"

"I dreamed it last night," Han said calmly.

Xander stepped forward and knelt beside them. He looked at the little boy with a warm smile. "What else did you dream about?" he asked.

Han seemed to look inward. "Just that there is the Light and the Dark. One of them always wins, but both are necessary. This time, it is different. One is trying to win forever. It is not allowed, but He does not care."

"Who does not care?" the wizard asked, eyes narrowing.

The little boy looked at the evil tree then back at Xander. "It is not who you think."

"Then who is it?"

"I am not allowed to say."

Xander tried to keep the irritation from his face. Chip had seen that look before. The others remained quiet, knowing this was somehow very important.

"Who says you are not allowed to say?" the wizard asked.

"Chip knows." Han looked up and grinned. The orphan was momentarily confused, but then an image formed in his mind. Could it be?

By now, Xander could not hold his frustration and let out a burst of pent-up air. "Well, my goodness. You two remind me of each other." He looked at them sourly. "Could either one of you care to elaborate?"

Chip looked at Han and started to smile. "What colour was the hair of the person who told you what you can say?"

The little boy gave a genuine laugh that made the others smile despite the moment's gravity. "Silver!" Now, it was Chip's turn to laugh. Soon, both were holding their bellies, doubling over.

Xander threw up his hands and began chuckling too. Eleanor covered her mouth as if it was improper for a princess to laugh excessively, but she could not help it. Auntie Clare grabbed Han and hugged him. The others enjoyed the respite from the recent dangers.

After a while, the wizard wiped tears from his eyes and looked at them kindly. "One of you will explain what happened one day. The best laughs occur when you least expect it." He patted Han's head. The boy beamed up at him, pleased he had made everyone happier, especially his sister, who now seemed content. "Is there anything else you would like to share?"

Han nodded. "There is something in the mountain."

Xander's mirth faded. "What is it?"

The boy shrugged. "Something that called to me." He tapped his small head.

"Did it say anything to you?"

Han laughed. "It wants to be found. It cannot speak, but it still talks."

"Ha. You are a special little boy, Han. The Dark Elf named Zoran looked into your head. Could you feel it?" The wizard leaned forward.

"Yes," Han replied, "He wanted to know about him." He stopped to point at Chip. "I did not let him. He wanted me to show him what Chip did to the black dragon, but I did not want to, so I got mad." He pretended to make an angry face.

"What did you do then?" the wizard murmured.

"I showed him how he would die."

The others looked at each other. The wizard covered his surprise with a cough. "And how will Zoran die?"

Han again pointed his finger at Chip. "He will kill him."

"Do you always see or dream these things?"

"Yes."

"Do they always come true?"

The little boy hesitated. "Mostly. But sometimes, no." He scrunched his face in thought, then looked around. His eyes lit up when he saw a faint trail leading to the clearing. "See, if I walk on this path, it will go to the bad tree. Another path may go to a different tree. If I see all paths going to the same tree, then it comes true."

The wizard pondered this. "That is very interesting, young Han. Do all paths lead to Chip killing Zoran?"

"Yes, now they do."

"Is the thing in the mountain dangerous?"

The little boy paused then nodded solemnly.

"Do we end up killing it?" Xander pressed.

"Depends which one."

The wizard's eyes widened, and he snorted. "That is the problem with Seers, or Tellers, if you will. The vagueness and possibilities shroud everything in mystery to the point where there may be no advantage. Their knowledge can even become dangerous," he warned.

"It is a balance," the little boy said.

"My goodness." Xander bent to study him. "I do not doubt you can see things, young Han. Perhaps you can do more. I want to see in your mind but cannot use my magic here. The ones on Cave Mountain may sense it. I hope the amount of magic Auntie Clare used to kill the Dark Elf was not sensed. Han, we will talk again one day, perhaps in Toron."

The boy looked at him sadly. "No, we won't."

The wizard gave him a long stare. "Do all paths lead to that?" he asked finally.

The boy seemed to look inward again. "Almost. Only one path does not."

"How does it happen?" the wizard finally asked.

"Not allowed," the boy said.

Xander sighed. "Ha. It is for the best, anyway. Alright, one last thing, my boy." He pointed at the ancient tree in the clearing. "Do you know what that evil thing is in the tree?"

Han nodded, and for the first time, his small face took on a look of fear. It was the only time Chip had ever seen him afraid. "Yes."

"What is it?"

The boy shuddered. "It eats the Paths. If it is released from the tree, it will hunt you."

"Then we will kill it," Xander responded.

"You cannot kill it."

"Why not?" asked the wizard.

"It is not alive. Your magic won't work."

"How do we stop it?"

Han shrugged, lifting his small palms upwards. "It eats the Paths. I do not know."

The wizard considered. "I have heard of such a thing once. Very well. You have given us much to think about. Please go with Auntie Clare and these fine men. They will take you and Beth safely away." He looked at the soldiers. "What are your names?"

The taller soldier stood straight. "I am Neb, and this is Jon." The other man acknowledged the wizard. They then turned to Garth and saluted. "High Commander."

The weapons master stepped forward and saluted back. "Take Clare and the children to safety. Guard them with your life. Spread the word that the demons are capturing villagers and bringing them here. If possible, have anyone going to Calgar do so in large groups, carrying weapons. A Dark Elf, even with magic, can only control so many." He looked at Xander. "Do we need the horses?"

The wizard shook his head. "They will be a hindrance in the caves. If we get through and make it to the other side of the mountain, we can continue on foot and get new mounts in the Witch Town of Banfar, north of Calgar." He turned to the soldiers. "Take our horses. We will give you what supplies we can. Wait until dark, then hug the forest line across the valley back towards Fang Pass. When Vanalon falls, leave Calgar before the demons arrive and bring the children to the safety of Toron. If anyone gives you grief in the capital, have a message delivered to the Wizard's Guild addressed to High Wizard Balor saying that Xandrostika guaranteed you safe harbour. My brother will then have King Dominor take care of you." The wizard reached into his pouch and gave them a handful of silver coins. "Complete your task, and you will get more in Toron."

"Yes, Mr. Wizard," Neb and Jon said in unison.

Garth Stone looked around. "We are near the edge of the forest. It is getting darker as we speak. Let's go a little further east to the edge and then part at nightfall." Xander agreed.

The companions surveyed the clearing, littered with dead bodies. The light was failing fast, and the wind had picked up again. The dark storm clouds refused to budge, hanging over the mountain like an overbearing parent. All were eager to put as much distance as possible between themselves and the evil clearing. The great tree in the middle seemed to leer at them grotesquely.

Chip took one last look at the red altar, trying to imagine how many sacrifices occurred over the millennia, and shuddered. They gave the three remaining horses to Aunt Clare and the soldiers. Han sat in front of Neb and Beth with the head midwife. Garth passed over some weapons for the men to use in case they encountered any trouble. If they did see any demons, the commander instructed them to gallop in the opposite direction.

The entire party continued east. Shortly afterwards, the trees began to return to normal size and finally thinned out. The sun dropped below the dark clouds on the horizon, and dusk settled in. Cave Mountain loomed over them like an evil hunchback. They kept hidden so that only the stunted peak of the mountain was visible. When they reached the forest's edge, the group hunkered down behind a thicket of pine trees and waited for the stars to come out.

The travellers talked in low voices of better times and places. Chip realized the enormity of what had befallen them in the last two weeks and knew that nothing would ever be the same again. He looked at the small group in the growing starlight and thanked the Creator that he had met such good friends.

When night fell, the weapons master signalled, and both parties rose to exchange farewells. Auntie Clare hugged Chip and wished him the Creator's blessing. He responded in kind. The boy shook the hands of the two soldiers, who looked at him in awe. He realized they had seen him destroy the black dragon in Vanalon before escorting Auntie Clare and the two children to safety.

They bowed low to him, which made him feel awkward, then saluted the commander. Beth came up and gave him a quick embrace, then Han leapt into his arms, hugging him tightly.

"You must find what's in the mountain," Han whispered in his ear.

Chip nodded, "I will. Keep Auntie Clare and your sister safe."

Han laughed, "They will be safe. See you in Toron, depending."

Chip grinned, "Yes, depending."

They laughed infectiously, causing the others to join in. The parties departed, waving farewell. The orphan watched as darkness enveloped the horses, then turned to face Cave Mountain.

4

The companions backtracked into the trees and headed north. After a short trek, the forest grew sparser until they had no choice but to leave its cover for open ground. A cool night wind buffeted them from the west as they stood exposed on a flat rock sheet. The air felt electric. They would not miss Fang Forest in the least. Looking east, Cave Mountain loomed like a dark monolith, taking up most of the horizon. A wide path led up to it, but Garth veered into a gully continuing north. From there, they followed several deep clefts in the rock that shielded them from prying eyes. After half a league, they swung around and came back towards the mountain from the north. The chances of discovery were much smaller from this direction.

From this angle, the party encountered a steep slope, but the weapons master found a thin, rocky path that meandered up the mountainside. Manipulating through the jagged steps took almost an hour of concentration.

Chip realized the horses would not have done well in this terrain. He was happy they were taking those he cared about to safety. Little Han's words occupied his thoughts. What Powers did the boy possess at such a young age? What was under the mountain?

He shuddered at the thought of going deep into the Demon King's three-thousand-year-old lair. He had no idea what to expect. Despite that, his priority was to find the other human captives Auntie Clare mentioned.

They were nearing the top of the steep hill when Garth signalled for them to halt. The group of five peered over the lip of the mountain to see the dark circular outlines of three caves, which overlooked the entire valley to the west. Fang Forest was now a dark smudge down below on their right. The wind changed direction and blew sideways from the caves, causing them to gag on the familiar demon stench. Several dark figures milled around in front of the entrances.

Without warning, a giant boom of thunder erupted overhead. The boy felt his heart skip a beat. A few moments passed, and lightning struck something near the top of the mountain's stunted peak. In the sudden flash of light, they had a clear, unobstructed view of the caves. Three giant black holes stared out like some strange multi-eyed creature. Six demons guarded the left cave entrance. They were of varying shapes and sizes. Two of them were on the ground, biting savagely into what looked like a human corpse. Chip felt his rage ignite and looked darkly at the wizard.

"Soon," Xander whispered. After the lightning disappeared, the wizard waved them down a few steps below the top of the slope so they could confer.

"There are six guards, two of them are…eating. The human prisoners will be in the cave behind them on the left. We will take out the guards first, then release the captives. I need to see their condition before deciding what to do next. The cave on the right leads to an eventual dead end and does not interest me. The middle cave was sealed three thousand years ago when the Unnamed One left his lair to fight the Great Battle. One hundred feet inside the entrance is a door warded with powerful magic. I need to see if it is open. No Dark Elves are in sight, meaning they could be in any cave. There is also a risk they have found the party of demons we slaughtered in the clearing.

"What was that thing coming out of the tree?" Chase asked. "It did not quite look like a demon and had no teeth or eyes. Something was all wrong about it."

The wizard looked at him, and any hint of warmth left his face. "That creature is no demon," he paused. Thunder boomed above him, followed by a jagged streak of lightning. "If it is what I believe it to be, then it is the most dangerous thing alive. The Demon King may subjugate the whole world, but this creature kills and destroys everything in its path. It literally eats life."

"Like Morgo?" asked Chip.

"No, Morgo pulled energy out of the life around him to animate his physical body. He used the power of Death to create black magic. This creature is different. Its touch is instant death. Any life form it makes contact with dies, but not just our human bodies. It takes away our very spirit essence forever. This means the tree it is crawling out of should also die. The fact that it does not terrifies me. It means that the Unnamed One has, through his runes and symbols, found a way to contain this creature of death or at least appease it with sacrifices. If he can command it, he has a weapon to destroy us all."

Chase raised his hands. "So now, instead of just the Unnamed One to defeat, we must avoid being hunted by something we cannot even kill?"

"Correct, our magic will not work on it. Nothing that we know of can kill it."

"What is it called?" asked Chip.

The wizard looked at him. "It is called the Dim."

"Have you ever seen it before?" Chip asked.

"No. If I had, I would not likely be here. A book in the old Wizard's Guild talks of this creature. Its creation was likely an aftereffect of the Great Forget, similar to Morgo, but much worse. It appeared in a valley far to the north in the troll mountains. A mage tried to kill it but soon realized it was his gravest mistake, for he gave the beast purpose. His magic did not affect the creature, so he tried to flee. It followed the mage, killing whole villages along the way. The creature almost singlehandedly wiped out the entire troll civilization.

In the end, all the troll mages still alive gathered to make a final stand and managed to defeat it."

"How did they kill it?" asked Chase, enamoured with the story.

"My goodness. Aren't you listening, boy?" He looked at Chase as if he was daft. "You cannot kill it, so they did the next best thing."

"Which was?" Chase waited, trying not to sound exasperated.

"They dropped a mountain on it."

"Huh."

"They literally dropped a mountain on it. The Dim was buried alive...or dead," he corrected, "if we are to believe young Han. The weight stops it from moving, at least for a while." The wizard paused for dramatic effect. "I wanted you to know this now in case you run across it."

"Is that supposed to make us feel better?" Chase asked in disbelief. "What do we do if we run across it?

"Run!"

"Really?" He looked startled and grinned. "As long as I beat Chip, I don't care."

"Very funny," the orphan muttered.

Xander rolled his eyes. "Alright, let's save these poor human captives from those foul demons. We will move after the next lightning strike. Try to come up behind the demon you select to kill. If we encounter any Dark Elves, try to incapacitate them before they draw Power. Use magic if you must. If we see Zoran, be wary; he is one of the Inner Circle, a dangerous one at that. The Unnamed One must have needed someone quite powerful to open the sealed cave if that is his purpose, or perhaps he gave him some sort of key. I do not know. We must work together to defeat him and any other magic wielders."

They nodded and moved back up the slope to peer over the top. The same six demons were in front of the cave on the left, but now two different ones were taking their turn chewing on the half-eaten corpse. The companions did not have to wait long before a booming peal of thunder sounded, followed by a long, jagged streak of lightning.

"Now!"

They all ran forward when the light disappeared, keeping low. Xander reached down and threw a rock over the demons' heads, creating a loud clatter behind them. The creatures all turned to look.

In moments, they were on them, driving daggers deep into the skulls of four of the beasts. The other two turned in surprise, letting out the beginnings of a snarl before Garth and Chase, reacting in a blur of motion, slashed their throats.

They scanned the area for more demons. The torches in the cave entrances illuminated them to anyone watching, but for now, they seemed unobserved. Xander ushered his companions into the cave on the left.

The group crept down a shadowy tunnel that went back about fifty feet before opening into a large stone chamber. They reached the cavern to find two heavily muscled demons guarding a dozen humans sitting in a circle on the floor. Their hands were tied. The creatures snarled and immediately moved to intercept them. The weapons master walked forward smoothly. He met them in the middle of the chamber, swinging his sword in a sweeping arc. The lead demon raised its arm to block the attack, but the blade sliced clean through its wrist, then continued into the center of the creature's face.

The second demon tried to leap at Garth from the side, but Chase intercepted it, driving the point of his sword straight into its sternum. The impaled creature snarled again, still trying to slash him, but he grabbed the hilt with both hands and pushed the sword deep into the thing's chest. It grinned wickedly at him before sinking to its knees. He placed his foot on its chest beside the blade and withdrew his weapon before decapitating the smiling creature. Its headless body fell backwards.

Xander approached the astonished humans, beckoning them to their feet. There were six men, three women, and three children. The smallest one was wailing in terror, watching the black blood leak out of both demons.

The wizard tried to reassure them. "They cannot hurt you

anymore, little ones." He and the others untied their hands. "Do you know where they put your belongings and weapons?"

The frightened group pointed to the chamber's far end, which wrapped around into another large room they had not seen from the tunnel. Walking around the corner, they were shocked to find human belongings going from floor to ceiling, reaching back thirty feet to the far wall. There was an array of clothing, weapons, and various travel items. It was obvious that many villagers had been captured and held prisoner in this cave. The victims were either eaten or sacrificed to the Dim in Fang Forest.

"Quickly, gather what you can. Find a weapon to defend yourself," the wizard instructed.

At first, the villagers tried to find their belongings, but they were only partially successful. The demons had tossed their possessions haphazardly into the immense pile so they could not retrieve everything. All the adults and children grabbed a weapon except the smallest one. The men preferred swords, while the women and children chose long daggers.

"We must leave now before they notice the guards are missing. Hurry," Xander urged. They escorted the villagers back through the stone chamber and rounded the corner to the tunnel.

Everyone stopped cold. The children screamed.

Blocking the tunnel at the other end was what could only be the Inner Circle member, Zoran. He wore a deep blue cloak that shimmered at the slightest movement. He had the white, almost handsome face of the Dark Elves. A rich mane of dark-brown hair surrounded his long, pointed ears. Zoran's black almond-shaped eyes made his whole countenance appear evil and demonic. On both sides stood an array of several lesser Dark Elves. Behind them, a dozen or so demons waited hungrily, some so tall their head and shoulders stood above those in front.

Zoran stepped forward. "It looks like you are finally trapped, Xandrostika. You do not understand how long I have dreamed of this moment." He smiled, and even that small movement made his cloak shimmer.

"Looks can be deceiving, Zoran. Perhaps you are the one who is trapped," Xander said casually.

A brief look of doubt crossed the Dark Elf's features as he considered, then shook his head. "You are bluffing, old man." He turned his gaze on Chip. "Is this boy really the last hope of humankind?" The elf emitted a deep laugh, which echoed off the tunnel walls. "My Master, may we grovel at his leisure, has changed his plans for you, boy. He was willing to forgive the foolish mistake of killing his black dragon and even look past Marta's death, one of his favourite Inner Circle pets, but what he cannot forgive is what you did to General Morgo. He was my Master's teacher and friend. For that, he has decided to release the Dim on you."

Zoran stepped aside, as did the Dark Elves and demons. Crouched on all fours in the cave entrance was the Dim, the same creature that had tried to crawl out of the ancient tree in the clearing. Chip felt his blood go cold. Everyone around him gasped.

Xander's face was one of disbelief. "How could you, Zoran? It will kill us all!"

The Dark Inner Circle Elf laughed again. "No, it will only kill the boy and whoever is with him. My Master told me how to control it. There is no escape from this cave, old man. One touch, and you die. It eats your very spirit essence. Your magic cannot hurt it. Your weapons cannot scratch it. Not even my Master knows what it is. Even he feared it. Morgo went to the mountain in the Troll Kingdom that held it down all those centuries to study it. He found it had burrowed its way up over hundreds of years and would have escaped on its own anyway. It would be the weapon that won the Great Battle for us. Then, my Master found the Orb of Power, so he did not need the Dim to win the war, yet he still desired to control it. He went to the Troll Kingdom and released the Dim using the orb to unearth it.

"Morgo found a way to contain the creature through arcane arts, imprisoning it in the ancient tree within Fang Forest. Then you, like the treacherous thief you are, stole our orb on the eve of the Great Battle and used it to push us back. My Master was going to retreat to the forest and release the Dim, but Arkan was clever and cut him off with the orb. We withdrew to what you call Demon Island. My Master also sealed the caves before the Great Battle as a precaution." He laughed to himself, shaking his head. The Dim sat at the tunnel entrance, unmoving. "You think my purpose here is to unseal the main cave. It is not. Only my Master has that Power. No, I was sent to feed the Dim and release it with purpose."

"You fool!" Xander shouted. "That creature is not a pet. It will end up killing us all."

Zoran smiled. "For three thousand years, the Dim has waited in its prison in Fang Forest. It has waited for a purpose." The Dark Elf pointed at Chip. "Its purpose is to kill you now, boy. My Master has trusted me to set the Dim free. I know how to control it. I am protected."

He beckoned to the creature, and the dark thing moved forward from the cave entrance on all fours. A fell dread descended over the tunnel as it approached. The demons pressed themselves against the walls, eyes full of fear. Some of them whimpered in terror. The Dim moved slowly, sniffing the air. Even the Dark Elves looked apprehensive and gave the creature as much berth as possible. It stopped in front of Zoran, looking up expectantly. The elf's blue cloak shimmered as he lifted a trembling arm and pointed directly at Chip.

"Kill him."

The Dim turned to look at the boy. Its eyes were hollow holes. The creature had a thin body with long black arms and legs. The material of its body looked strange, almost metallic. It was like a single piece of metal. There was nothing alive other than its movement. Its gaze made Chip shake with fear. He had never felt anything like it. The mouth opened and revealed a black, gaping hole with no teeth.

It then uttered a sound that filled everyone present with despair. Even Zoran shrank back. The otherworldly moan came from a place no living creature had ever been. It seemed to destroy all hope. Some of the villagers broke down in tears. The demons started raking their skin with their claws. One collapsed and slid down the tunnel wall, scratching at its eyes. Chip felt a hopelessness like never before. The sound spoke of the eternal, vast emptiness of true nothing.

Yet again, even as the thought entered his mind, he heard the very distant voice of the weapons master. "Don't give up." He remembered making a promise to himself that he never would. Knowing it was hopeless, he vowed to fight anyway. To access his magic, the boy thought of the Dim hurting the princess.

His rage immediately ignited, and Chip blasted through his Wall, filling himself with Power. His eyes blazed bright red.

Zoran staggered back at the sight. The Dark Elf must have heard of the boy's magic but still thought him weak. Seeing him now, filled with unbridled Power, made the Inner Circle member appear uncertain. The elf's eyes moved back to the Dim, and then he relaxed, for the outcome was not in question. There was no hope for them.

Chip watched the creature walk disjointedly down the tunnel. It did not take its hollow eyes off him. As it approached, one of the village women could not take the despair any longer and decided to run past the Dim to the cave entrance. The thing did not even look at her as she ran past. It simply reached out with one elongated arm and touched her exposed skin. She stopped moving instantly, her body crumpling onto itself, lifeless. It continued moving without slowing.

Chip's mind raced in shock as he thought of how to escape. He decided to test the legend himself.

Lifting both hands, the boy blasted red fire down the entire tunnel. He saw Zoran raise a blue shield and leap behind the Dim to protect himself. The Dark Elves followed suit. The demons in the back were not so intelligent, and those on the sides burst into red flames. The Dim merely walked into the fire untouched. The red Power dissolved when it reached the creature. Those behind the beast remained unscathed.

Chip's fear grew, even while holding the Power. His determination began to waver. He had never seen his magic have no effect before. The Dim kept coming forward. The boy thought frantically of how to escape. Even as he deliberated, another villager broke down in fear and tried to sprint around it. The creature again reached out, caressing the man's neck, and his face went slack. His feet stopped moving, and the villager fell face-first onto the stone floor, dead. More screams erupted from the others. Chase and Garth had their swords out. The Dim was almost upon them.

Chip thought about dropping the mountain on it then instantly realized it would kill them too, even if he could pull off such a feat. It was too late anyway. The creature was before them. The weapons master leapt forward and brought his sword down with two hands on the creature's head. A metallic thud sounded, and sparks flew off his sword. The Dim did not slow. It shot out a hand, and Garth barely pulled back in time through well-honed reflexes. The creature's black hand raked the blade of the Protector's sword just above his fingers.

Chase came in and swung down on the thing's extended wrist with all his might. Incredibly, the Dim's arm did not even drop from the impact. Sparks flew off the blade. As soon as the sword hit its arm, the creature swung its hand sideways to touch Chase. It caught his cloak as he raised his hands to avoid the lethal swipe, tearing the cloth. Luckily, it did not touch his bare skin. The creature kept its eyes on Chip, who was now within range.

Fear coursed through the boy, and his magic wavered. He retreated until his back was against the room's stone wall. The others had managed to move to the sides out of reach, but Zoran sent a ball of blue fire at them. Xander erected a shield in haste to protect the humans.

Chip tried one last thing. Raising both hands, he levitated two of the largest demons from the middle of the tunnel and shot them forward with frightening speed. The Dim was only a few feet away from him. He placed the demons on either side of the creature and pressed them together against the beast's sides, lifting with his Power. It worked. The Dim's feet left the ground as the pincer movement carried it into the air. He pushed it backwards twenty feet, then watched in horror as it sank back down. The demons died instantly upon touching the Dim's sides, and then their bodies blackened and turned to ash. They disintegrated before his eyes. Chip had nothing to use to pincer it anymore.

The Dim landed on the ground and continued walking towards him as if nothing had happened. Its hollow eyes never left him.

He looked up to see Xander throw a blue fireball at Zoran. The Dark Elves added their green fire to Zoran's blue shield. Desperate, Chip levitated two Dark Elves and whipped them forward, placing them on both sides of the fast-approaching creature. He lifted the Dim off the ground again just before it reached him. An elongated arm flew out with black fingers extended. He felt the wind from its fingertips as it swiped in front of his face.

The Dark Elves writhed in pain as he crushed them against the sides of the Dim. Their clothes prevented a direct touch, so they did not die immediately. Shrieks of terror escaped their lips as they struggled to avoid touching the beast with their bare skin. Chip pushed the creature down the tunnel towards the other end. The Dim reached up and touched the faces of the Dark Elves pressed against its body. They both died on the spot. It kept its black hands pressed against their skin, which started turning black. Chip only had moments before they were ash.

Throwing his Power forward, the boy used the dead bodies to fling the Dim into the rest of the demons and Dark Elves still in the tunnel. Zoran pressed himself against the stone wall in time to avoid contact. The others were not so lucky. The creature careened into them, its touch killing a few of the Dark Elves and several demons. It came to a stop then stood back up and sniffed the air before turning to stare at Chip. The Dim then resumed its disjointed gait towards him.

Zoran waved the remaining demons and Dark Elves out of the tunnel. He did not want more bodies used as pincers to levitate the creature. Chip could not reach them with his magic as the Dim blocked them from his view. The remaining villagers screamed and cried as they watched the unholy creature descend on them once more. The three children clutched each other in terror.

"Get to the sides out of its way," ordered Garth. Chase made sure everyone moved to the side of the room. Chip stepped back until he touched the far wall, drawing it away from the others.

"Get around it when it comes for me and run down the tunnel," Chip yelled. They started to protest, but he cut them short. "There is nothing you can do. No weapon or magic can hurt it. I have a chance if I am alone. Do not argue. Go!"

They nodded as the Dim entered the large chamber, coming straight for the boy. The others were able to run around the beast and race down the tunnel to the cave entrance. Eleanor stopped halfway, turning back with a look of anguish.

"Go!" he shouted. "You can do nothing here. Help Xander fight Zoran!"

She nodded, tears sliding down her cheeks, and turned to follow the others. The wizard was already fending off a renewed attack by the Inner Circle member at the cave entrance. The villagers huddled in a knot behind the old man.

The Dim came forward relentlessly.

Chip had never known such frustration. The creature was unstoppable. He stared at its hollow eyes and looked into the depths of despair. Fear took away his hold on the Power, and the Wall reappeared. His magic was useless anyway. He watched as everyone he cared about ran away from him. It swept him back to when he was a little boy and had no friends. The orphan felt as alone as ever. The Dim walked the final steps towards him.

Out of instinct, he darted sideways as it swung out a long arm, barely missing him. He was almost able to make his way around it, but the creature stepped sideways like a crab, cutting off the angle. As it closed on him, he darted the other way at the last possible instant. This time, it was ready and raked its hand out, catching the boy before he slid past.

Chip knew he was dead as it touched him, yet the nails of its right hand only caught his tunic, tearing it open. The hand felt like a hard diamond, but the cloth saved him for the moment. Seeing his exposed flesh, the Dim reached out to touch his bare skin. This time, it was a hair off as he slipped past, following the wall the other way. He let out an explosive breath, realizing he was not dead yet.

The boy tried to run down the middle of the chamber to reach the long tunnel, but again the Dim was already sidestepping, cutting him off. The sounds of its hands and feet slapping the ground as it stepped were metallic and hollow. The orphan had no choice but to run to the room with the sacrificed villager's belongings. Now, he was truly at a dead end.

The Dim came on without hesitation. Most of the lessons Chip had learned over six years of training were useless here. He could not attack it physically. His Power, which saved him many times before, was impotent. The creature was impervious to magic. He felt utterly alone and defenceless. There was no escape. He screamed at it in frustration.

The Dim opened its mouth and let out a moan so horrifying that he knew life was over. Despite his best efforts and everything he had achieved in his short existence, it was all completely irrelevant. The sound drained the energy from his very soul. He stared into its hollow eye sockets and wondered why he had bothered to try.

Chip's life flashed before his eyes. He saw himself as a little boy standing forlornly before Miss Stern, getting scolded, so exhausted he could barely stand. Then he stood before King Barton, who labelled him a demon that needed banishment. He remembered lying feverish on his bed in the stable, ready to give up on life. Next, he was standing in front of the signal fire with blood dripping out of his many wounds before he fell into blackness. The boy saw himself on a battlefield, watching the black dragon snatch Han and Beth's parents in its jaws. All those memories proved what life was really about.

It was all death and misery.

He saw this in the Dim's vacant eyes as it closed the distance. His last memory was of Morgo, made of Death itself, trying to kill him.

Something stirred in the orphan. For some reason, he needed to know how that memory ended. The throne room appeared, and he remembered Morgo hurting the princess. His mind jerked awake as a jolt of anger shook him.

He remembered Eleanor struggling as the general tried to snuff out her life with his black magic. Rage filled him. A final image of a man with silver hair made him realize there was always hope. He broke through the Wall and filled himself once more with his Power.

The Dim was in front of him. He leapt back as it swiped, landing on a pile of belongings. Chip scrambled backwards as it continued forward, going up the hill of the dead villagers' life trappings. He reached the top of the mound. The Dim climbed up, disjointed limbs moving like a four-legged spider. It slipped on some items that could not bear its weight but continued crawling towards him. He had nowhere left to go. It was almost there.

Knowing he would die, Chip decided to discover what this creature really was. With eyes blazing red, he surrounded himself with the Calm and inserted his presence into the Dim's mind. Immediately, the boy entered an alien landscape of thoughts and memories. Time slowed. It made no attempt to block him. Why would it? It had nothing to fear. The Dim was not designed that way. He examined its first memory of where it came to be.

The Dim did not know how or why or what it even was. It was just there. The sky above it was erupting in a fantastic explosion of colours. It moved its new body, not sure what to do. The colours died down in the sky, and it decided to explore. It touched stone as it walked and then descended into a valley. The creature sniffed the air and smelled something interesting...a temptation.

It followed the scent to a green bush. It did not know what it was, but the smell made it reach out and touch the leaves. Immediately, the bush turned brown and disintegrated, but a tiny bit of energy was absorbed into the Dim. It liked the feeling of the energy. It sniffed again and found another intriguing scent. This time it was a tree. In its primal mind, the creature did not understand words, only images.

It did not need words. It reached out again and touched the tree. The green leaves withered, and the bark turned black. Curious, it kept its touch there, and the whole tree disintegrated into ash. A bigger jolt of energy coursed through the Dim. It decided it liked touching things. From then on, it kept walking through the valley, touching everything until nothing was left.

Chip watched as the Dim remembered a troll entering the dead valley and sending a stream of green magic at it. The creature did not know it was a troll but understood that the being was more alive. The green fire felt like nothing, so the Dim ignored it. It decided it wanted to touch this new being. It sniffed and liked the smell of this new life form. It followed the troll relentlessly. When it entered a village, it followed the troll but touched anything nearby. It learned to touch bare skin over clothing. The first troll villager it touched gave it a jolt of energy like no other, and it desired more. It finally found its true purpose. Eventually, the Dim cornered the troll mage and touched him, feeling exhilaration. It decided that it liked trolls and chose a new target. It never stopped until its target was destroyed.

The Dim continued following the trolls and touching them until it began to run out of these beings. Finally, it saw many of them gathered at the top of a valley. It desired to touch them all. It descended into the valley to cross to the other side. When it reached the valley floor, the creature watched as a great display of colours exploded from the hands of the trolls on the valley ridge.

It reminded the Dim of the colours when it first came into being, except there was no red here. Something immense fell on the creature, and it could not move anymore. It did not care. The Dim knew it would get out and touch them. Time meant nothing to it. It was able to move its finger, and it started scratching at the hard substance that had buried it. It scratched and scratched until finally, after an unknown period of time, it could move its other fingers.

From there, it was able to use its whole hand to scratch and then its arm. It continued for many memories until finally, it could scratch with both hands and pull its body upward. It continued this upward scratching and crawling for an indeterminate period and then felt something draw it out of the ground.

It emerged into daylight to see a being with red eyes lift it by pressing rocks against its body. He was holding a glowing white stone in his hand. The rocks moved it to a spot where the Dim could place its feet on the ground, and then they fell away. Some other being that looked like a snake stood with the red-eyed one. The Dim sniffed the air and decided it wanted to touch the two beings. The one with the red eyes had a unique scent that excited the creature to touch it.

It began walking forward, hollow eyes fixated on the one with red eyes. Then, the snake being walked right up to it and stopped. The Dim reached out and touched the snake's face. Something strange happened. It did not die. Instead, a jolt of pain went through the Dim. It had never felt pain before and did not like it.

The snake being entered the Dim's mind and told the creature that the red-eyed one would always give it fresh beings to touch. The ones it liked. If it ever tried to touch the red-eyed being, the snake would touch the Dim and give it the pain it did not like. The Dim never forgot the first pain and never needed to be taught again. It was told to always listen to the red-eyed and snake beings.

The snake also explained that the red-eyed being could give instructions to the Dim through other beings, and it must listen to them. Sometimes, it would have to wait for instructions.

After that, the red-eyed being gave the Dim many beings to touch. This happened for many memories. Chip felt nauseous watching the creature touch humans and even lesser demons. The amount of life this creature took was staggering. One day, the red-eyed being told it to stay in the tree in the clearing of a forest. Marks were inscribed on the tree, allowing it to hide there. There were other beings in the tree on the other side of a veil or curtain. It could not touch them physically, so it ignored them.

An indeterminate time passed, and then a being called Zoran came to the tree and began feeding it again. Zoran showed the Dim a memory of the red-eyed being, giving him the authority to issue instructions to the creature. The Dim would not touch him. It would only follow instructions. In return, it received fresh beings to touch. The beast made sure it always followed instructions, or else it knew the snake being would give it pain, and it did not want that.

Chip felt a jolt of shock, realizing that the Dim was being controlled by someone who was dead. He immediately showed the Dim his own memory of killing Morgo.

"You do not have to listen to Zoran or the red-eyed being

anymore. The snake one is dead and cannot hurt you," Chip said in the creature's mind.

Incredibly, the Dim stopped moving as it pondered this new information. It realized it could now touch whatever it wanted. The creature had no sense of happiness or indebtedness. It could only think in terms of pleasure and pain. It knew no more pain was coming, so it could touch everything it saw again. It sniffed the air, and then the hollow eyes locked on Chip.

To the Dim, this red-eyed being smelled like the other red-eyed one. They must have the same thing inside them. It carried a strong temptation.

The boy released his presence from the creature's mind, grunting in frustration. He was hoping that the revelation of Morgo's death would somehow spare him from its obsession with taking his life. It continued climbing up the dead villagers' belongings. The boy shuffled back until the cave wall pressed against him. He had nowhere to go. Chip would be dead in moments, in the most total sense. He knew this creature would not just end his life but also take away his very spirit essence. It eats the Paths, as Han said.

The Dim reached out to touch him. In desperation, filled with his Power, he thought of Eleanor and knew what his final act would be. He would make sure the Dim would not be able to harm anyone else. He released his Power straight up into the cave ceiling above him. The roof imploded and then collapsed in a jumble of broken stone. Instinctively, he surrounded himself with a thick aura of red magic. Chip watched as the stone above fell on both of them. He felt it press down on his body like an immense, immovable weight.

The boy maintained his aura of red Power, watching the stone beside his body melt. His magic was a bubble that protected him, but he did not know how long he could maintain it. Eventually, he would run out of Power. As the stone melted and reformed, it exposed the Dim's black hand, which appeared right before his face. If the boy leaned forward even a little, he would be dead.

In a panic, Chip pushed back as hard as he could, slowly melting the rock behind him. He felt some give, but even as he did, the Dim's hand began to move and continue reaching for him. Its main body was still trapped under huge boulders, but the stone around its hand had melted away. He changed course and moved sideways, melting the rock with his Power. He had to hope the main chamber had not collapsed, or he would not make it back to the cave entrance. The boy had no choice but to slide around the Dim to return to the main chamber.

Even as he did, Chip watched the stone melt around its metallic body, freeing its left side. He pushed harder as it tried to move towards him. Its leg swung and brushed his shoulder, just missing his exposed neck.

The rock finally melted and separated, then opened into the chamber. He fell onto the stone floor. The room was still intact. The roof had only caved in above the villager's belongings. He gasped in relief and released the red aura enveloping him to conserve his Power. The boy breathed in the fresh air and relished the openness after being entombed in solid rock.

A metallic sound behind him made his stomach lurch. Chip spun around, watching in horror as the Dim manoeuvred its way into the crevice he had created by melting the stone with his magic. Only its right leg was still embedded in the rock, but even as he watched, the Dim pulled hard several times with inhuman strength until the rock encasing its leg broke away with a loud crack. It fell on its back on the stone floor and then righted itself like a spider. The creature sniffed the air, and the hollow eyes fixated once more on the boy. The Dim started moving towards him. Chip thought of bringing the roof down again but did not want to trap himself, so he did the only thing he had left.

He ran for his life.

Bolting through the main chamber, he entered the tunnel and sprinted headlong towards the cave entrance. He heard metallic thuds as the Dim gave chase. He should have used caution, but in his need to escape the unrelenting creature, the orphan ran full speed out of the cave entrance onto the side of the mountain.

He was greeted by a ball of blue fire from Zoran, who hid with a group of Dark Elves inside the entrance of the third cave. Chip dove to the side and broke through his Wall to surround himself with a red shield. He felt blue heat on the left side of his body, but it neutralized quickly.

Scrambling behind an outcropping of rock to his right, he found his wide-eyed companions huddled together tight. Chip released his shield. Eleanor squealed and hugged him with tears in her eyes.

"I was so worried," she mumbled. He hugged her back, remembering how he thought he would never see her again only a short while ago. His eyes still blazed red.

"How on Earth did you kill that thing?" asked Chase in awe.

"Simple," Chip said, extricating himself from the princess. He pointed at the cave entrance. "I didn't." The Dim appeared in the tunnel's opening even as he said it. It sniffed the air and stared at him. "I have an idea."

"My goodness, you better make it snappy!" the wizard exclaimed with a look of disbelief. "I do not know how you made it out of there, but we need to do something fast." He glanced at the Dim, who was already bearing down on them.

Chip turned, filling himself with Power. The creature released a low moan, sending a jolt of terror through everyone. A ball of blue and green magic hurtled towards them from Zoran's direction. He waved his hand in annoyance, sending the ball careening harmlessly into the side of the mountain, lighting the night sky.

Extending his arms, Chip lifted two large rocks in front of him and sandwiched the approaching Dim between them. He raised the beast off the ground and floated it towards the third cave entrance. Zoran's face turned to one of shock, then horror. The Dark Elves beside him shrieked with fear.

When the Dim reached the opening, the boy pushed hard with his Power, sending it and the rocks hurtling through the entrance. Immediately, screams echoed off the tunnel walls as the creature went to work.

He looked at the others. "It will come back for me. We need to go." Chip realized he was still holding his Power and let go. When he did, a small wave of dizziness hit him, but he brushed it off.

Xander looked at the terrified villagers. "This is your chance to escape with your lives. Follow the trail down the mountain, keeping the forest on your right. Do not enter it unless you see approaching demons or Dark Elves. Even then, stay near the perimeter until they pass. Cross Fang Pass at dawn. You will be safely out of these cursed mountains by late morning. Let the other villagers know that no one is safe and to travel in large, armed groups when possible." He looked at the three terrified children. "Stay strong, little ones." They nodded, and the adult villagers thanked them then descended the mountain trail.

The wizard looked at his companions. "Get into the main cave entrance. Our only chance is to lose it in the tunnels." They all sprinted for the opening. Horrifying screams continued to erupt from deep within the third cave.

As they entered the main entrance, Chase and Garth grabbed two lit torches stuck in mounts on the wall. The light revealed a long tunnel with two immense, gilded gold doors at the far end. All along the tunnel, depictions of demons fighting men in great battles were carved into the rocks. The companions all ran, taking in the images as best they could.

When they reached the gold doors, the final depictions on the tunnel walls showed the Demon King standing on a hill of human skulls, wearing a crown. He was holding a sword in one hand and the Orb of Power in the other. The Unnamed One's face was chiselled perfection. His whole aura, even in stone, evoked immense power. Chip realized he was standing at the front doors of the home of the most feared being in the world.

Xander walked up and pulled on the door handle to the right. A brief crackle of Power sounded, and the wizard flew backwards, landing on his rump.

"Well, my goodness. Same thing happened three thousand years ago," he grumbled, getting up while rubbing his backside. "You would think I would have learned by now."

"Great. So how do we get in?" asked Chase. They could still hear distant screams outside the cave entrance, which they all tried to ignore.

"Good question, for once." Xander looked at Chip. "Please try opening it."

The boy nodded. He thought of the Dim coming down the tunnel and trying to kill them all, and his rage ignited. The weariness disappeared as he broke through his Wall, and the orphan drew in his Power.

He pushed out with his presence as if he were entering another mind. Chip wrapped himself in the Calm to ensure complete focus. His presence entered the doors, and he felt a shield of Power. It was like a woven red blanket that infused the solid gold of the doors themselves. The shield was anchored into the tunnel walls on either side. He instinctively knew that no magic below Red Level, or possibly the Orb of Power, could open it.

A sudden scream erupted from the cave entrance.

"No!" It was Zoran. Chip pulled his presence back and turned, red eyes blazing. The Inner Circle member ran into the tunnel with one Dark Elf following close behind. The Dim chased both. The others drew their weapons out of instinct, knowing they were of little use. Xander's eyes blazed bright blue.

"What did you do to it?" shrieked Zoran, running towards them with a blue shield.

Chip stepped forward. "Oh, nothing much. I only showed the Dim that Morgo is dead and that it does not need to listen to the Unnamed One or his disciples anymore, which includes you."

Zoran's face went ashen. "But how..." he sputtered. A scream sounded behind him as the lesser Dark Elf stumbled and fell. The Dim was on him in moments. It touched the exposed ankle of the elf, who stopped all movement and fell face forward on the stone. The creature crawled over him without looking down. Its metallic hind foot landed on the back of the dead elf's head, pulverizing his face into the stone, making a loud crunching sound.

Zoran screamed again, running towards Chip with hate. "You will all die, too!"

"No, just you." Chip strode forward, lifting both hands.

A sudden recognition crossed Zoran's face as he looked at the red-eyed boy striding towards him, as if he had seen what was about to happen. "No. It can't be!" he screamed. Chip's anger flared. This Inner Circle Elf had killed countless villagers and unleashed a terror on the world. He blasted through Zoran's shield as if it were thin paper and picked him up off the ground.

"Put me down," Zoran shrieked. "My Master will kill you all!" Chip threw both hands forward, flinging the shrieking Dark Elf straight at the oncoming Dim. The creature did not even need to raise a black hand. Zoran landed on the Dim's head, and his cry was cut short. His body shrouded the creature's face for several moments before turning to dark ash and falling away. The Dim did not even slow.

Chip turned back to face the gold doors and took a breath. The creature was closing the distance fast.

"You might want to hurry," Chase offered, voice quavering.

Chip reached out, placed his hand on the right door handle, and pulled. Nothing happened. His eyes blazed bright red. There was a momentary pause as the shield stopped him. Then, recognizing his red Power as if he was the Unnamed One himself, the shield dropped, and the door opened.

Xander exhaled in relief. "Quick. Run through!"

The Dim arrived as they slipped through the door, reaching with its black hand. The weapons master went last, trying to pull the heavy door shut in front of its outstretched metallic fingers. With no room to spare, the door clanged shut.

A loud thud sounded immediately from the other side as the creature tried to force the doors open. The main latch held for now.

"Drop the bar," yelled Chase as he held the door while the others lifted a heavy bar up and onto the mounts spanning both sides. It slid into place as the rhythmic thudding continued. They watched as the doors buckled after each impact and the hinges vibrated.

"The Dim will break through," Xander stated wearily, "It will not give up until it does." Chip released his Power, feeling lightheaded. He wobbled momentarily, but Eleanor was there to grab his elbow. "It seems the magic seal on the door was one of recognition. The seal is now gone. Only the bar prevents entry. At the time, the Demon King had no reason to suspect someone else with red eyes walked the Earth. He likely assumed the Red-Eyed King was confined to the Ancient City. He also did not expect to lose the Great Battle. A simple recognition seal allowed the doors to open upon his return, but it was nigh impossible for others. A weaker wizard could not open it, even linked, as the seal does not recognize anything less than the Red Level. The orb might have circumvented it, but the Light Elves had taken it with them."

The rhythmic pounding continued unabated.

The wizard turned around and examined the tunnel leading downward into the mountain. "For three thousand years, this cave has been sealed. Let us find out why."

5

The wizard strode forward with a determined look in his eyes. Though they carried torches, Xander lit a blue ball of light that floated a distance in front of them to provide more illumination. They all marvelled at the strange beauty the receding darkness revealed.

The tunnel was perfectly hewn into a rectangle with immaculate corners at every angle. The floor had a shiny, waxy substance, shimmering even beneath a thick layer of dust. Ancient paintings pilfered from countless cities and villages over the centuries lined the walls. The ceiling had more intricate stone carvings of battles depicting the Dark Elves as victors.

It was hard not to feel a sense of power and importance emanating from the tunnel, but something else was there too. It was more a feeling that seemed to exude from the stone itself. It was a sense of evil and malice that superseded all. The sounds of the Dim striking the door muted to a dull echo as they descended the sloping tunnel deeper into the mountain.

Something shiny glittered at the outskirts of the blue light. Coming closer, they entered a large foyer with two monstrous silver doors. To the left and right, the tunnel branched off into dark openings.

Xander's eyes blazed blue, and then he signalled to Chip.

"There is a similar shield on this door. I suspect it is to keep everyone out unless the Demon King is present." Chip nodded and embraced the Power. Shattering his Wall was almost automatic now, as he knew what thoughts ignited his anger. The thrill of the Power erased his weariness for the moment.

He walked forward and pulled the large ornate handle of the door on the right. It resisted a moment, then the ward recognized his magic, and the immense twenty-foot-tall door opened soundlessly, light as a feather.

Chip entered first, feeling a great sense of openness as he walked into the darkness. His steps echoed. The light streaming through the door brightened a large floor area, but only when the wizard threw the ball of light forward did the enormity of the room materialize. They all gasped as one. The ceiling rose a hundred feet above their heads, filled with gigantic stalactites. The floor looked inlaid with a mosaic of gems shining below the layer of dust. Thick bronze pillars spaced twenty feet apart ran down the center of the monstrous room, supporting a lower ceiling of silver carved with symbols and runes. The pillars focused the eyes straight ahead to a large, high-backed diamond throne sitting atop a series of gold steps. They walked forward in amazement.

Xander's face held a look of awe. "Even I who have seen most of the known lands of Amrika have never gazed on such a wonder as this." His eyes blazed as he sent his magic out. "This throne is quite possibly the most valuable artifact in the world. I have seen several diamonds throughout my life, none bigger than a filled wineskin, but this is a..." He paused as his eyes blazed again. His voice took on a note of disbelief. "He cut it himself with his Power from a single diamond. Where he found such a thing, I do not know. Even a Blue Level cannot cut a diamond."

Lifting his hands, the wizard lit up the entire room. The stone walls at either end were covered with gorgeous paintings bordered by luxurious drapes. Long, rectangular stone tables lined the walls on either side with iron rings drilled at regular intervals above them. Their wonder turned to disgust as they realized the pale white things on the tables were ancient bones.

Some human skeletons, still wearing tattered clothes, were stuck in the rings on the walls. Others had slid through the shackles as their flesh disappeared to collapse into a pile of bones and garments. The Demon King must have left them alive when he departed from the caves to fight the Great Battle.

Other skeletons could only be the lesser demons that the stronger ones fed on. Several had multiple limbs at odd angles to their torsos, indicating they were mutant demons to be used as fodder for the stronger ones. The tables were stained a dark red from centuries of feeding and torture.

They turned back to the center of the room, faces grave. Walking forward, the group approached a long gold table with seats for fifty on either side. Each spot held a complete set of silverware covered by three millennia of dust. This was where the Dark Elves feasted while the demons ate humans and their lesser brethren on the sides. An eerie quiet filled the room, punctuated by the incessant pounding of the Dim on the entrance doors. Chip realized that no human had ever gazed at this place and survived.

As if reading his thoughts, the wizard proclaimed, "We stand in the Great Hall of the Lord of the Dark Elves and King of the Demons. No human has beheld this lair of evil and lived to talk about it. This place has been frozen in time for three millennia. Everything is exactly as it was when my father, High Wizard Arkan, used the orb to banish this demon threat from the world." He paused, his voice getting quieter, eyes looking off in distant reverie. "This time, we cannot banish them. We must kill them all."

Xander walked around the gold table and stood before the dais, beholding the diamond throne. Light brown dust covered it from top to bottom. His eyes blazed, and with a swipe of his hand, the dust flew off the chair. In that moment, they beheld a sight none would ever forget.

The throne seemed to explode with shimmering bits of silver light in a glittering myriad. Even the slightest move reflected new light from different angles until it looked like a dazzling waterfall.

"It is beautiful," the princess murmured in awe. "A piece of it could buy a kingdom."

"Great. So, let's break off a piece, then be on our way," Chase said to no one in particular.

Eleanor gave him a withering look. "Its true value is leaving it as a single piece. Sadly, the most valuable thing in the world was created by the most evil thing. How can such beauty come from something so dark?"

Xander answered, "It did not. The Demon King did not create it. The Earth did, and the Earth came from the Creator. The Dark Lord may have sculpted this, but the Creator forged it. No taint of evil permeates this diamond. It reflects all. The very stone in this room oozes evil, but not this throne. One day, we will seize it, and a human king or queen will sit on it."

"Well, that's assuming we can escape that deranged creature pounding on the front door," Chase added. The pounding ended in a sound of tearing metal and then a loud clap as something very heavy struck stone. Everyone looked at each other, knowing that sound could only mean one thing. "Well, that's awkward," Chase squeaked.

"Help me bar the throne room entrance," Garth ordered, moving swiftly to the silver doors. They had not noticed when they entered, but a huge silver bar rested in an alcove to the side. They ran for it, realizing the Dim was coming down the hall and would be at the doors momentarily. Chase reached the alcove first and pulled the enormous bar down, letting the others slow its descent. It took all of them to carry it towards the door. They could hear metallic steps coming closer on the other side. Chip's heart quickened as he remembered the feeling of helplessness that the Dim generated in its victims. A hungry moan erupted in the tunnel beyond, growing in volume as the Dim approached. The inhuman noise reverberated off the stone walls. Their faces turned white.

They were almost there. As one, they lifted the bar to slide it in place, but there was a massive crash as the Dim barrelled its body into the silver doors. The primary latch cracked, and the doors buckled. The right door opened enough to knock them backwards. They tried to hang on to the heavy silver beam, but their balance was off, and it toppled over their heads as they fell.

There was another loud thud as the Dim struck the right door again, opening it this time. It stood in the doorway on all fours, gazing at them with hollow eyes. The very light and life of the room seemed to dim in its presence.

It sniffed the air then locked its hollow gaze on Chip, who lay on his back, frozen in fear. The boy forced himself to scramble backwards, trying to reach his feet as the creature advanced.

Suddenly, Chip felt the crackle of magic and turned to see Xander standing with eyes blazing blue. The wizard extended both hands and pointed at the heavy gold bar, which lifted off the ground, hanging suspended in midair. With a grunt, the wizard swung both hands sideways, and the heavy beam followed suit, flying with stunning velocity straight into the torso of the Dim as it entered the room.

The sound of the beam hitting the creature was like a giant steel mallet striking an anvil. The Dim flew backwards through the door, flipping over repeatedly before striking the stone wall at the far end of the large foyer. It fell to the ground but immediately righted itself and turned towards the throne room entrance. The creature began advancing without hesitation.

Xander, hands still outstretched, floated the bar back inside the room, then slammed the door closed in the face of the oncoming creature. He dropped the beam into place. The wizard lowered his hands and released his Power, breathing heavily. Almost immediately, they heard the Dim strike the door. The main latch had broken, but the bar kept the enormous doors securely in place, for now. The rhythmic pounding started up again.

The wizard surveyed the doors. "This will hold it for a while. We must go now and see what else is in the mountain. I sensed something below me when I used my magic, something sentient. Be careful and follow me."

They did not need to be told twice.

The group passed the diamond throne again, watching it sparkle in a shower of light. Chip wished he could stay and marvel at its beauty but then glanced at the iron rings lining the sides of the room, some still occupied with various types of skeletons, and decided he would rather be elsewhere. A strange foreboding hung heavy in the air. The clanging on the throne doors only added to the sense of dread. The Dim scared him. It was something worse than Death. It was an alien thing that ate everything in its path. He was no closer to figuring out how to stop it. Even as he thought about how to escape such a creature, the pounding ceased. They all turned to the doors in fear, but they were secure. The group looked at each other and waited, but the banging did not resume.

Chase looked around happily. "That should be the end of it, right? I'm sure it has finally given up," he nodded, hoping the others would agree.

Chip looked at his friend without amusement. "It will never give up, ever. I looked into its mind. It is a dead creature with limited understanding and no communication abilities. It only knows pleasure and pain. When it has a purpose, nothing will ever stop it. There must be a reason it ceased knocking." Chip drew his brows together in concentration, and then his body went cold with realization. "We need to move fast," he urged. He started to jog to the back of the throne room.

"What is it?" asked Xander, keeping up on his left. The others kept pace. Behind the throne, they crossed a large open space to reach a bronze door.

"The Dim smelled a faster way," the boy said to the others. "It sniffs the air and then follows our scent. Two tunnels branch out from the main foyer. It seeks to take one and then intercept us as we exit this room. All I know is it did not stop or give up. It found another way."

"I believe you are correct. Let me take the lead," Xander reached for the bronze door.

"Wait," Chip said. "This door is likely sealed too. Let me go first."

The wizard closed his eyes for a moment, then opened them and nodded.

"There is a ward. How did you know?" he asked, puzzled. "You did not use your magic to sense it."

Chip shot him a quick smile. "Logic. The Demon King would not want anyone sneaking behind his diamond throne."

"Ha. Quite right."

The boy broke through his Wall with red eyes flaring, pushing the door open.

"Be careful," the wizard warned. "The Dim could be anywhere."

Chip stuck his head out, revealing a long, dark hall. Xander ushered a small blue ball ahead of them to provide some light. The hallway was covered in bronze from floor to ceiling. The metal had dulled to a dull green over the ages, and the dust was thick beneath their feet. Chase sneezed into his arm. The others shushed him. The group proceeded quietly.

A large door across the hall was engraved with a helmet, indicating the room was important. Chip sensed a seal and opened it with his Power, revealing what could only be the Demon King's bedroom suite. The room was immaculately appointed, with a giant four-poster bed cradling a feathered mattress. Chase reached out and pushed down on the intricately embroidered coverings, which collapsed to dust. The wood holding up the bed groaned and cracked, and the whole structure fell in on itself. He stepped back to avoid inhaling the plume of dust that erupted from the pile. Chase looked at the others sheepishly. "Oops."

The wizard rolled his eyes. "Let's hope the Dim cannot hear well."

"It has no holes for ears, so I doubt it," Chase tried to sound convincing. Xander shook his head in resignation.

The room contained old tables, mirrors, and chests. Chip stood in front of a full-length mirror, realizing that the Demon King had stood in that very spot three thousand years ago before setting off to fight the Great Battle. The Unnamed One was likely convinced he would win, given his possession of the Orb of Power.

The bedroom suite contained smaller adjoining rooms, some

holding archaic costumes and suits of armour. There was a black, horned helmet resting all by itself on a shelf of gold that gave the boy chills. Various weapons from different lands and eras adorned the walls. Paintings long dulled by dust and time had frames that weakly shone of gold or silver. Each item looked to be priceless, but nobody disturbed a thing. A pall of evil hung heavy in the air, imbuing the objects and surroundings with a foul taint.

Chip vowed that one day, if they defeated this threat, the artifacts would be returned to their rightful homes or displayed in places for all to see. The princess and wizard did not need money or gold beyond using it to carry out their duties. To the orphan, each item initially seemed like an end to poverty and hardship but his training had taught him the dangers of living a life only seeking material luxuries. The inherent human need for greed always needed taming. Material possessions could become an end in itself, becoming some people's only purpose in life, regardless of who they step on. As the weapons master said, in the end, it was not what you achieved that mattered but who you became. Despite that, Chip thought it would be nice to experience luxury at times.

Growing up, he did have moments of jealousy for those who never had to suffer hardship, yet the weapons master made it clear that those who struggled received the greatest reward. They were the ones who learned and appreciated the most in life. As Garth also said, there was nothing wrong with being wealthy if it did not make you soft and selfish. Much good can come from wealth if used responsibly.

The Unnamed One was a collector of these rare items. Chip felt it had more to do with taking what belongs to others instead of amassing wealth. The Demon King wanted control over all, whether it be material possessions or lives. His addiction was power and control in all its forms.

For Morgo, his whole life consisted of getting more Power. He even gave his spirit essence to do it. Chip shook his head at the sheer insanity of such a trade. Did people really need everything while others had nothing?

He realized with a start that all the artifacts before him were frozen pieces of time. Each represented a creation or belonging of another person now hidden deep within the Demon King's lair. What stories they could tell, he thought.

The Demon King's bedroom suite had a back door, which the boy used his Power to open, listening for the Dim. Hearing nothing, he opened it farther and peered down a hall that bisected the first one—at the end stood large double doors engraved with an ominous symbol of crossed swords cradling a horned helmet. They traversed the hall and opened the doors to reveal a large oval table made of gold resting in the middle of the room, surrounded by lavishly padded chairs, all pushed in. It was the Demon King's council room.

Detailed maps covered the walls with points of colour depicting important cities and borders. Xander examined them up close. Chase reached out to touch one, but the wizard slapped his hand away.

"One day, they may be salvageable or worthy of historical study. One press from your finger, and this parchment will disintegrate. Keep your hands to yourself," Xander admonished. He approached the most extensive map depicting the Great Plains west of Toron. "This map represents the final war plans used by the Demon King before he attacked the combined armies of the Light. I see a dot where the battle took place on the Great Plains, with the words 'The End of Humankind' inscribed." Xander ran his finger across to Toron and showed surprise when he found another inscription. "The End of The Red-Eyed King" and "The Great Forget."

He then traced a line north to the old Wizard's Guild at the southern edge of the Troll Kingdom. The writing below the dot where the old Guild was located read "Arkan's Prison" in bold letters. Chip looked at the wizard in surprise.

Xander's eyes blazed blue with raw anger. "He was going to imprison and torture my father in the Guild's fortress," he said, his voice trembling with rage.

Chip had never seen the wizard display such unbridled emotion. It was a rare instance of him losing control, but he understood why. Xander, despite his recent warning to Chase, pressed his finger on the spot where the words were written. Immediately, the writing disappeared in a puff of dust. Chase was about to say something, but the weapons master elbowed him, shaking his head.

The wizard stood for a few moments before the fire left his eyes.

"Let's go," he said. They hurried across the room and stopped in front of the door at the far end. Chip, using his magic, released the ward.

"Quiet." Xander turned the door handle and cracked it open to peer out. It opened to a much larger hall. Their hearts skipped a beat as they heard metallic footsteps echoing through the tunnel. It was hard to tell exactly how far the Dim was from their location, but the sounds seemed somewhat distant.

Pressing his finger to his lips, Xander moved to the right, opposite where the sounds emanated. They followed him, trying not to make noise. Garth made sure the door did not make a sound as he closed it behind them. None knew if the Dim could hear, but they were not taking chances. Chip realized that even if they were dead silent, the Dim could smell them. As the thought entered his mind, the footsteps stopped. They all froze in fear. A few moments later, they resumed, quicker this time.

The Dim had picked up their scent.

The wizard increased his pace and turned left at the end of the hall. It began to descend here, and the paintings and furniture became sparser. They peeked into a few of the doors lining this tunnel, which revealed comfortable rooms but much less lavish. Articles of clothing inside revealed that these were quarters for the Dark Elves. The tunnel went on for a good distance without an end in sight. To their dismay, the metallic thuds grew in volume. The Dim was getting closer. They were about to break into a run when the light revealed an end to the tunnel at a large iron door which stood ajar. A foul stench emanated from the opening.

They went through the door without considering their options and pulled it shut. There was no bar for this door, but it only opened outwards, and they did not feel the Dim was intelligent enough to turn the handle and pull it towards itself. Its only thoughts were to move forward and touch its prey. The tunnel they were now in bore downwards into the mountain.

There was no ornamentation in this area of the caves. The walls were roughly cut into the bare stone. They took a moment to investigate a few dark openings off to the side and discovered small rooms with bones of different sizes littering the floor. The smell was so repugnant that it was difficult not to gag.

This could only be the demons' quarters where the naked creatures lived and ate their weaker siblings. Demons were born with a primary desire to feast and conquer. In general, they did not need material items, clothing, or bathing. Some had rudimentary speech, but that was where their intelligence seemed to end. However, selective breeding resulted in unique characteristics that gave them threatening attributes.

The sound of metal on metal stopped them in their tracks. The Dim had found the iron door. Immediately, a rhythmic banging began, which they knew would not cease until the creature found its way in. The party quickened their pace as they descended deeper into the mountain. The number of rooms on either side seemed endless. Some were much larger than others, indicating demons bred for size. One cavern held schoolbooks arranged on a table, which had disturbing implications. Could the Dark Elves have bred some of these creatures to read?

The feelings of dread and hopelessness magnified as they descended deeper. So much evil and death had resided in these tunnels over the millennia, it felt like a palpable thing. Chip tried to imagine the rooms filled with all shapes and sizes of filthy, naked, hairy demons tearing at human flesh or their lesser brothers. The grunts, shrieks, and mewls would be a constant cacophony of madness and despair. The feeling of the entire mountain pressing down on him as they descended into the bowels of the Earth began to weigh on him. At least the metallic thuds were growing more distant, but what would stop the Dim after it broke through the iron door?

"Quick question," Chase asked. "How do we get out of here?"

The wizard looked at him sideways. "Good question. I am

working on it. Going back the way we came does not seem an option, as something particularly intent on killing us is in that direction. I remember from the wizard histories that there were possible exits on the east side of Cave Mountain leading to the plains. These were observations made by a Light Elf scout after the Breaking and never validated. If I recall, it was only a footnote of no real import in the stories. When the Unnamed One left Cave Mountain to fight the Great Battle, historians assumed the demon hordes exited the caves on the west side. They went south to the One Road or circled the mountain to enter the Great Plains. Openings on the mountain's east side would certainly not be big enough to march an army through. Then again, if it was mentioned as a footnote, it is likely true, but judging by the foul air down here, it is difficult to imagine that it opens to the other side."

"So to summarize," Chase offered, "you are taking us down here on a hunch, based on the observation of a single Light Elf made over three thousand years ago that an exit exists on the east side of this cursed peak, and if you are wrong we are all likely going to die at the hands of a demented creature that sucks the life out of everything it touches, including our spirit essence, as it chases us down to a very dark end in the bowels of the most feared mountain in all of Amrika?"

"Yes. That is exactly right." The wizard smiled in appreciation. Chase's eyes widened, and the weapons master grunted.

At that moment, a distant metallic tearing sounded, followed by an audible thud. They all knew what that meant.

"It is coming," Xander intoned, his face turning serious. "We must make haste." His eyes blazed blue, and he looked at the boy. "I sense something below us but cannot identify it. Chip, can you try? Imagine sending out your Power not to strike but to sense."

The orphan felt unsure but nodded. He broke through the Wall and drew in his magic, feeling an instant thrill as his weariness disappeared. Chip forced himself to focus on his surroundings, wrapping himself in the Calm, face serene.

With eyes closed, he sent his magic out in all directions. Behind him, he sensed the oncoming Dim. It did not have a life signal that he could identify like his companions but instead displayed a complete absence of anything. It was like an empty hole moving down the tunnel behind them. It was still quite distant.

Something else called to him though. He moved his presence ahead of him and then downward, lower and lower, until he felt a life form. There was more than one. He gasped at the power of the life essence below him. He could not tell if it was a monstrous evil or a loving being. He only knew it was pure energy. He pulled his presence back, searching for a path to the power. He opened his eyes and looked at the wizard.

"I think I know where it is."

"Lead the way, young man."

Chip set off at a brisk pace down the tunnel. He felt the princess move beside him, squeezing his hand. He looked at her reassuringly and did not let go. The tunnel finally ended, splitting in both directions. Without hesitation, he turned right. The boy had released his hold of the Power but still had a rough drawn map etched in his memory. Unfortunately, the air quality continued to deteriorate. The tunnel continued downward at an even greater angle. The openings on each side were extremely rough-hewn.

They decided to examine a few of them, experiencing instant revulsion. Inside were dank rooms with iron rings affixed to the walls. Some were empty, but others held the remains of three millennia-old humans. Their skeletons still had wisps of tattered clothes and hair draped over their brittle bones. Skulls looked at them with vacant eye sockets. The Demon King had left them in these dungeons to rot while he fought the Great Battle. He knew he would have many more humans for his demons to feast upon when he was victorious.

Chip tried to imagine the feelings these people had in their final moments, locked in the bowels of Cave Mountain, surrounded by various forms of black-eyed demons. Some of the skeletons had an arm or leg missing, meaning the demons would tear a limb off as a snack before coming back later for more. With horror, he discovered some of the skeletons could only belong to small children. A festering rage began to develop in the boy at the thought of these abominations running rampant in Amrika, capturing frightened women and children. The number of demons that could fit in Cave Mountain staggered him. There must be thousands of such rooms.

They hurried on, knowing the Dim would not take any breaks. The dank tunnel branched again, and he continued to the right. More passageways and rooms appeared as they travelled steadily downward. The air grew cooler and damper. The stench began to lessen, replaced by a smell of sulphur, which was not much better. The tunnel's gradient became steeper as they descended.

"Wait," Garth cautioned. They all stopped, listening. Faintly, they heard a steady metallic thud. The Dim was getting closer. "Keep moving. Let's hope there is a door somewhere."

Chip continued choosing the direction, always following a descent. The tunnels were rough-hewn as if a giant had made a few lazy slices to create a vaguely rectangular passage. Finally, the tunnel ended with no branches. It stopped at the top of rough stairs, like natural ledges leading down into the darkness. They stopped momentarily so Xander could send a ball of light downwards. The sound of the Dim's footsteps became louder. It was likely only a few hundred feet behind them.

"Quick," the wizard urged them on, his voice betraying a tremble of fear. The Dim was not just something that could kill them. It would eat their very spirit essence as if they never existed—it ate souls.

They tried to race down the steps. Some of the stairs had two-foot drops. As they progressed, the stone became slippery and covered with greenish moss. The smell of sulphur increased. The air felt more chill and damper. Chip slipped once but caught himself on the slimy wall. As he did, a moan erupted from behind him, making his heart freeze. The Dim was on the stairs, closing in. They threw caution to the wind and took the steps as fast as possible.

The princess stumbled, but Chip caught her before she landed on the hard rock. Chase then slipped on a particularly slimy step, which sent him down a few ledges on his rump. He got up immediately and looked accusingly at the stairs. It would have been comical, but for the gravity of the situation.

The sound of metallic clanging on stone increased. They began to panic. Evidently, the Dim's four spider-like legs allowed it to descend much quicker than they could. Garth positioned himself at the back with a grim expression, knowing he would be touched first.

They scrambled as fast as possible, slipping and sliding but staying on their feet. The stairs wound downward in concentric circles, surrounded by wet stone. They felt like they were in a vertical coffin. The Dim was now only a couple dozen steps behind them. Total fear set in as they leapt down the endless stairs. A burst of cold air from below signalled they were close to something. Then, the Dim caught up to them.

6

A clang of steel on metal sounded as Garth turned and struck the creature with his sword. It reached out to touch him. That gave the others the chance to descend a few more steps. Suddenly, the stairs ended, and they flew headlong onto a rocky beach. For a moment, nobody seemed to understand how it was possible. Then Chip realized they were at the very bottom of Cave Mountain.

Above them, like a cone, the sides of the mountain rose to dizzying heights until it terminated in a small circular opening of light. In front of them was a small lake surrounding a tiny island.

They were in the center of the mountain. The flat, open top of the stunted, misshaped peak allowed light to penetrate from above, like the opening of a volcano.

They scrambled to their feet as Garth continued slashing at the Dim, dodging its outstretched hands. This served to slow the creature slightly as it twisted and turned, giving the others time to run away. Unfortunately, they were confined by the thin, rocky beach surrounding the small lake.

The companions turned to their right, sprinting as fast as they could. Chip looked at the small island in the middle, realizing this was where the sentient life he sensed resided. In the center was a triangular diamond with no windows, a solid piece similar to the Demon King's throne. He looked back to see the weapons master disengage the creature and run after them. The Dim gave chase.

Chip envisioned the human skeletons hanging from the walls, allowing his rage to manifest. He broke through his Wall, eyes blazing red, and surrounded himself in the Calm. The boy scanned the beach and walls of the mountain, seeking a way to cross the lake. He knew they could swim it, but something told him not to. The water looked almost black with a heavy green tinge. The smell of sulphur was overpowering.

They were barely keeping ahead of the Dim, which could traverse the rocky beach quickly. He could not find two rocks large enough to pincer the creature. Eventually, they were going to tire and succumb to its deadly touch. Panic began to push in on the edges of the Calm. He could see Xander with eyes blazing blue, looking for options. They began to round the far side of the lake, hoping to find something to hurl at the creature. He glanced sideways and looked at the princess running beside him. He saw her eyes blaze a ferocious brown. She looked at him, then turned and stopped.

"No," he cried. "Keep moving."

She shook her head and faced the oncoming Dim. Lifting her hands, Chip felt the peculiar crackle of Power. Eleanor turned to the lake and reached out, pulling up a huge funnel of water. Spinning her hands, the stream of water rotated faster and faster. She waited until Garth sprinted past her, and then it was only the petite princess facing the implacable Dim. It rushed at her, reaching out a long arm. Bringing her hands sideways, she slammed the spinning funnel of water into the creature before it could touch her, flinging it into the mountain wall.

A loud metallic clang sounded, and chunks of rock flew off the inside of the mountain as it struck. The Dim landed on all fours, unscathed. Holding her hands in a vice grip, she wrapped the creature in the funnel of spinning water, lifting it again off its feet.

Eleanor then flung it sideways deep into the lake. There was a loud splash as the Dim sank like a stone. She released the rest of the water, letting it fall back down. They all stood there looking at her in a new light.

"That's one way to do it," Chase said in amazement.

Eleanor took a breath then turned to the others. "There's something in the water. I sensed it when I created the funnel," she warned. Even as she spoke, they could see ripples forming in different parts of the lake.

Suddenly, a dozen triangular heads broke the surface, revealing long, serpentine bodies. They were enormous snakes with menacing blood-red eyes and long forked tongues, flitting out between curved fangs. Their bodies rose fifteen feet above the water and likely a similar amount below. As one, they hissed and dove towards them.

Chip and Xander had already grasped the Power while the princess maintained hers, hands raised. In one smooth motion, Chase and the weapons master pulled their swords and held them aloft. Near the shore, the water erupted as multiple snake heads appeared, launching at them with fangs gleaming.

Xander created a blue shield to block the strikes, setting several serpentine bodies on fire. The creatures wriggled back to the water to put out the flames. A few went around and struck at the two sword-wielders from the side. Lesser men would not have been able to move in time to avoid the blinding speed of these serpents, but both men turned in a blur, bringing down their swords on the necks of each creature, shearing through flesh and spine. Shorn heads fell and rolled while the bodies spasmed on the beach. One of the tails whipped sideways in its death throe and caught Chase in the stomach, flinging him into the water.

Garth jumped forward and tried to grab the tall boy's collar, but another serpent wrapped itself around Chase's body. He pried his sword arm free in time before the snake dragged him under.

"No!" cried Chip as he watched his best friend disappear beneath the surface. He had been trying to reserve some of his Power for the

Dim, but now he had no choice. Stepping forward, he lifted his hands, but the princess stepped in front of him.

"Let me," Eleanor said with blazing eyes. She raised both hands and then separated them. The water lifted and formed a curtain on both sides, exposing the lake bottom beneath. Chip marvelled at the Power she displayed. He knew the Brown Level had a strong connection to earth, wind, and water, which she demonstrated impressively.

Chase struggled on the lake floor with the gigantic serpent. He was already sawing through the snake's enormous body with his sword. His arm was the only thing he could move. The tall boy's face turned purple from the pressure of the snake's coiled body, but with a few final saws, the serpent fell into two pieces. He staggered upright and then stumbled towards them.

"Can you maintain the curtains of water to the island while we cross?" Xander yelled. The princess gritted her teeth and nodded, then walked forward while raising the water until it formed an open-roofed tunnel to the island. "Hurry," the wizard yelled to the others.

As the companions ran across the exposed lake bottom, two huge serpent heads burst out of the walls of water on each side, trying to strike them with their fangs. Chase managed to dodge and slice the head off one while Garth impaled the other under its chin. A dozen other triangular heads suddenly appeared, but Xander formed blue shields along both sides of the walls, decapitating all the snakes that extended past the water curtain. His face strained from the effort and concentration.

They all ran forward across the bottom of the lake, dodging falling serpent heads. The ground rose upwards as they approached the small island.

Eleanor's face set in deep concentration as she held the water back. The lake floor was primarily bedrock below the mud, so they did not sink too deep. Chip remembered the deadly frog lake in Fang Forest, which would likely have a bottom consisting of several feet of mud, acting like quicksand. Xander's blue shield dropped as the group reached the dry ground of the island.

The princess stepped on the edge then staggered as she released the water, which rushed back in to fill the void. Chip put his arm around her for support, urging her forward. They looked around, ready to defend against leaping snakes, but none materialized. The water subsided until it was calm. It seemed the serpents only bothered those on shore, not the island.

The boy scanned the rest of the lake, wondering if the Dim was crawling somewhere under the water. Perhaps it could not swim, and the water destroyed it, but he knew not to put his faith in such a conclusion. "Prepare for the worst," the weapons master always said. "That way, you will never be surprised."

The princess leaned on him.

"Thank you, we needed that," he whispered to her with a smile.

She flashed him a tired grin. "It is the least I can do."

He turned to the structure in the middle of the island. "Now, let's see what is so important that it is protected by a solid diamond on an island, in a lake, under a mountain."

They all strode up to the triangular piece of stone roughly half their height. The wizard tentatively put his hand on it and closed his eyes. Chip saw a brief blaze of blue beneath his eyelids.

"This is indeed a diamond. Incredible!" Xander said in awe. "First the throne, and now this?" He looked at Chip. "My Powers are weakened for now. Can you make anything of this?"

Chip looked at the diamond and thought he could see something through it. He was about to extend his presence into the sparkling stone, but a splashing sound caught his attention. The Dim's head appeared out of the water on the other side of the island. The creature's eyes locked on Chip's, and then it let out a low moan. The hair on the boy's arms stood out.

The Dim emerged from the water, climbing onto the shore like a demented-looking spider. With a jolt of fear, the boy realized they were now trapped in the middle of the lake. After parting the water, the princess looked too tired to save them, and Xander was spent. Chip did not know if he had much left either.

"Focus, boy!" the wizard commanded. "See what is in the diamond."

The orphan looked down, knowing there was little time before the Dim reached them. He touched the cool stone with his hand and sent out his presence, delving into the gem.

He entered a hollow space in the middle of the diamond and then sensed two sentient beings of immense power. Surprised, he almost threw up a shield. "There are two beings in there," he announced to Xander. "What would you have me do?"

The wizard frowned. "My goodness, try to get them out."

He looked at Xander in disbelief for a moment, then focused on the diamond, which humans considered the hardest substance on Earth. The boy drew in his Power, feeling the thrill of energy, and probed around the structure, realizing in surprise that it was one solid, sealed piece. How could that be?

He raised his hands and directed a concentrated stream of red fire at the top corner of the diamond. At first, nothing happened, but then it sliced through. The life forms in the diamond responded to his use of the Power, one threateningly, and the other seeming quite amused by his antics.

"You may wish to hurry," Chase said offhandedly. "It's coming."

Chip realized it was taking too long, so he increased his Power and sliced the top of the pyramid off, ensuring it did not strike any life forms. Xander ran over and pushed the sliced lid all the way over, then gasped. Chip looked into the diamond, eyes wide.

On the base of the floor, nestled on a red cushion, were two eggs, one white, the other black. He felt an immediate aversion to the black egg, but the white one seemed to soothe him. Without even thinking, the boy reached down and grabbed the white egg.

"Careful," the wizard warned, but it was too late.

Chip held the egg in his hands, feeling like he was holding something powerful and precious. His presence reached into the egg, and their minds touched. The boy felt a rush of memories. He soared over snow-capped mountains amidst the thrilling rush of wind in his ears, drowning out his screams of joy.

The Dim appeared beside the diamond.

"Chip! Look out!" screamed the princess.

Mesmerized by the egg, he could not turn in time. The Dim was already upon him, reaching out. Eleanor leapt in front of the orphan, and seemingly in slow motion, the creature changed course and reached for her exposed neck.

Chip half turned, seeing the Dim's long finger about to touch her skin. He knew he could not reach her in time. His mind howled in rage and frustration. He watched as the creature was about to make contact. Yet before it could, the presence in the egg recognized his frustration and realized how much he cared for the girl. It linked with his mind, yanking her back in time with their combined Power. The Dim's fingers touched air, and it turned its hollow eyes on him instead, letting out a long moan. Clutching the egg protectively, Chip leapt backwards, out of reach.

Without warning, he felt the life form in the egg use their combined Power to dig under the Dim's feet and lift the creature upwards. The beast flew high into the air, projected by the ground itself, and landed on the other side of the island. A thought of running flashed through Chip's mind from the linked presence, and he looked at the others.

"Run!" he screamed.

The boy felt an incredible symbiosis with the life form in the egg as more images entered his mind. He saw a vision of another tunnel to the shore and, without thinking, used their combined Power to lift the water on both sides, as the princess had done. Chip lined the sides of the curtains of water with red shields of Power to ensure the snakes would not attack. The boy paused momentarily, realizing they had left the black egg, then saw the Dim coming around the diamond in pursuit. He shook his head in regret and ran after them, knowing there was no time to retrieve the other egg.

They ran across the lake bottom to the rocky beach on the far side, and Chip removed the Power holding back the water. The Dim was over halfway across when both sides of the lake came crashing down on the creature, and it disappeared.

Even after the expenditure, he still felt full of Power and could not believe how much magic the being in the egg contained. When they were safely on shore, they all looked back, looking for signs of the beast. Chip knew it would crawl along the bottom and reappear on the beach if they delayed.

With a gentle mental prod, the life form tugged on his mind, showing him a picture of a hole ahead of them in the cavern wall. Motioning the others to follow, the boy ran around a rocky outcropping on the mountain wall and found stairs leading upwards. He would have never seen it if not shown.

Chip looked at the others. "I do not have time to explain now, but I know how to get out of here. Follow me."

The wizard looked at him with mouth agape but they all nodded as the boy sprinted up the stairs leading the way. The stone steps were rough-hewn, winding upwards in circles. They were on the opposite side of the lake from the stairs they descended from, which meant they were on the eastern side of Cave Mountain. Now, they needed to find an exit ahead of the Dim.

After a short period of climbing, the companions heard a sound below them. It was metal on stone. The Dim was ascending the stairs. Chip clutched the egg, still linked with the life form. He thought of the black egg for a moment and wished they had more time to grab it, but the Dim had appeared, forcing them to run. Something about the black egg bothered him. The energy from the life form inside felt wrong. He would talk to Xander about it later if they survived.

Both the wizard and Eleanor had spent much Power. Chip felt strongly linked to the egg but knew that the Dim would eventually have them unless they figured out how to stop it. He pushed his thoughts aside and ran up the stairs as fast as he could, with the Dim giving chase.

They ascended upwards until their legs screamed. The sound of the metallic thudding of the Dim grew in intensity. It was adept at climbing, given its four spidery legs. Their fear began to mount. If the Dim trapped them in the stairs, they had little chance. Even as the sobering thought entered his mind, he felt a draft of warm air blow on his face. They were getting closer to some opening. He pushed them even harder. The orphan could hear Xander and the princess's laboured breathing. They were not used to such exertion. Garth and Chase kept up but even they displayed a sheen of sweat.

The sounds of metal on stone increased until the Dim was only a dozen steps behind them. The winding stairs seemed to have no end. The metallic scraping was so loud that their time left had dwindled to mere moments. Chip risked a glance behind and caught glimpses of the Dim appearing on the lower stairs below them. It began to reach out. They were not going to make it.

A black hole abruptly appeared before him, and there were no more steps to climb. They all tumbled out onto a rough passageway. Xander threw the blue light ahead of them.

"Run," Garth ordered. They sprinted down the dark tunnel, not knowing where it would lead. Even as they took off, the Dim burst through the opening behind them, narrowly missing Chase as he brought up the rear. Everyone ran in a panic. Chip knew they would tire at some point. It was just a matter of time.

He marvelled that the wizard and princess could keep such a pace but knew they were near exhaustion. Going full speed, they managed to put some distance between themselves and the creature. The Dim could not go as fast on straightaways, preferring to climb over uneven ground.

The passageway sloped upward for a long while before finally ending at a passage that flowed left and right. Without a thought, Chip went left. The life form seemed to tug him that way, and he knew that going upward would make the most sense. He suspected that turning right would lead back down to the demon caves. The Dim was a distance behind them now, but they could still hear the jarring sound of metal striking stone. The companions slowed a little to catch their breath. A waft of warmer air struck their faces, giving them some hope.

They followed the slope upward for a long period, pushing themselves hard. Time lost its meaning. All they knew was that the tunnel had begun to widen, and finally, it opened into a huge cavern. Moonlight peered through cracks high up in the ceiling between large stalactites, causing them to gasp in relief. They were close to a way out.

The weary companions crossed the large natural chamber to the other side, where the tunnel picked up again. The walls pushed in, funnelling them forward. Xander sent his blue light ahead to reveal what must be an exit to the east side of Cave Mountain. Instead, a pile of rocks blocked the tunnel and any hope of moving forward. They all stopped in shock.

"Well, that's not good," Chase said.

Chip thought of pushing forward with his magic through the stone, but he sensed at least fifty or a hundred feet of rock in front of them. Someone had sealed the tunnel on purpose long ago, making sure no one could ever come through this way again. Their only option was to backtrack and try to find a way out higher up in the cavern towards the moonlight.

"Go back. Let's climb up the cave and find an opening to slip through," Chip urged. The life form with him exuded agreement.

They rushed back into the chamber as the Dim arrived on the other side. Chip screamed in frustration and saw how tired the others were, all because this creature's only purpose was to destroy them. His rage began to mount, but he held his magic in check. The life form in the egg held up a mental image of a hand, signalling he should wait. He felt a slight tug left.

"Follow me," he told the others.

A natural ledge was next to the blocked tunnel opening leading upwards along the cavern wall. He moved quickly, picking his way around rocky outcroppings while mindful of where to place his feet. The ledge rose fast, and soon, they were over forty feet above the stone floor. He turned to see the Dim leaping onto the ledge. Chip looked down and regretted it.

Ever since he fell out of a tree when he was a boy, he was not fond of heights. Prince Rupert had leapt up and tugged on his foot while he stood on a branch. It was not a long fall, but it instilled an unnatural fear of heights in him.

He saw moonlight coming through the rocks another forty feet above. They continued on the ledge as it wound around the cavern, but it ended about twenty feet short of their goal. They would have to climb up the rock wall to reach the moonlight. Chip suppressed his fear and grasped an outcropping above his head.

A sharp scream from the princess echoed behind him.

"It's here."

The orphan let go of the outcropping, landing back on the ledge with eyes blazing. The Dim had climbed disturbingly fast and was closing in on Chase, who brought up the rear. Lifting his hand, Chip pointed at an enormous stalactite far above his head and ripped it off the ceiling with his Power.

The cone of rock broke with a crack, and Chip flung it with deadly speed at the Dim as it tried to touch Chase. The point struck the creature on the shoulder making it strike the wall and rebound off the ledge. They watched as it fell to the ground sixty feet below. Several loud metal clangs sounded as it landed on the hard stone then tumbled over a few times before stopping.

Without pause, the thing stood on all fours and swivelled its head until it locked eyes with Chip. A long moan erupted from its black mouth, sending chills throughout the whole party. The Dim scuttled towards the ledge to climb again.

"Quick, we must get to an opening," Chip said. He turned and grasped the rocky outcropping, pulling himself up. It was difficult to manage, but there were tiny ledges and other outcroppings to put their hands and feet on. As he neared the top, he grasped a projection of rock that broke off in his hand. He teetered for a long moment, hanging with one hand, trying to regain his balance.

He could swear the egg nestled in his side bag swung forward instead of letting its weight dangle behind, which would have caused him to fall backwards. He regained his equilibrium, trying not to shake or look down. The boy grabbed a different outcropping and continued pulling himself up. He could feel cool, fresh air strike his face. Above him was an opening. Chip grabbed the bottom of the opening and pulled himself up the rest of the way, ready to crawl into the night air. Instead, he exhaled in frustration.

The opening was misleading from the ground. It narrowed for twenty feet before exiting the side of the mountain as a fissure. Chip was not sure if they could even squeeze through. Since there was little standing room before the fissure, he moved to make space for the others.

Looking over, the boy saw the Dim reach the ledge below them. Chase was the last to climb and was only halfway up when the Dim leapt up and grabbed his foot. Chase wrapped both hands around a rocky outcropping and hung on with the creature attached. His muscles bulged as he strained with all his strength. The weight of the beast's metallic body must have been enormous.

Chip seized another stalactite with his Power and hurled it at the Dim, but the rock broke into pieces on the creature's body as it held on with a vice-like grip. Chase looked up into his best friend's eyes. For a moment, it looked like he could hold on, but the weight was too much.

"It's alright," he called, face straining. "It's been quite the adventure." Chase's hands slid off the rock, and his best friend fell off the mountain towards his death below.

"No!" Chip screamed. In slow motion, he watched Chase fall over sixty feet. Filling himself with magic, still linked to the life form, the boy threw their combined Power at his friend, stopping Chase's body before it hit the ground.

The Dim, still holding onto the tall boy, struck the ground first and released its death grip. Unfortunately, it bounced up off the floor in front of Chase. At the arc of its bounce, while hanging in the air, the black creature reached out to touch his face. Chip wrapped his friend with Power and yanked him backward in time to avoid the long fingers, then set him down.

Chase landed on his feet, looking at his hands and body in shock, realizing he was still alive. He let out a whooping laugh and sprinted again for the ledge. The Dim struck the ground with a metallic thud then turned first to look up at Chip and let out a horrifying moan. It then skittered after the tall boy.

Chase sprinted around the ledge inside the cavern then jumped to grasp the rocky outcroppings without hesitation, climbing to rejoin the rest of the party.

"Did I miss anything?" he asked, breathless.

Chip grabbed and hugged him, trying to keep tears from his eyes.

"You aren't getting out of this that easy." He couldn't help but smile at his bigger friend. Then he turned to the others. "Please crawl out of this forsaken mountain. I will go last."

Nobody argued. The opening was wide, but to get out, they needed to crawl on their hands and knees and then lie flat to slide between two huge slabs of rock to reach the open air. Chip turned to watch the Dim make its way along the ledge. He shouted at it in frustration. The creature, eyes fixed on him, opened its black mouth and moaned again. The inhuman sound spoke not just of death but a complete emptiness so profound that it robbed one of hope itself.

The life form in the egg responded with an anger the boy had never experienced before. He knew the Dim would be on them shortly. Chip turned to watch Xander slide out on his belly through the narrow fissure, followed by the princess. Garth and Chase were next. The orphan tried to crawl into the opening, watching as the weapons master struggled to get out.

"Give me your arms," shouted Xander in a muffled voice. "I will pull you through." He heard grunting, but it seemed Garth was stuck.

Chip turned to risk one last glance over the edge and saw the Dim begin climbing the vertical wall below them. A fresh wave of fear struck the boy, and he decided to go out of a smaller opening on the left to give Garth time to squeeze through the other one. Chip crawled as fast as he could on his hands and knees towards the moonlight, now giving way to dawn. He felt agitation from the life form in the egg at his decision, but it was too late.

He scrambled towards the narrow opening out of Cave Mountain in mounting desperation. Then, the top of the flat rock above him pressed on his back, forcing him to slide the last ten feet on his stomach. He was almost there. Three feet in front of him was the opening. He inhaled the fresh, cool night air. The stars were fading fast as dawn broke over the horizon.

The orphan had a brief surge of happiness as he realized they were on the correct side of the mountain facing east. He pushed forward again, then stopped in horror. He was stuck. Chip realized the opening here was much narrower than the one his companions were using on the right, but it was too late to go back. He had miscalculated.

A surge of fear flew through him. He pushed harder and felt the solid, flat sheet of rock below him press tightly against his stomach. The sheet of rock above pressed down on his back. Two feet in front of him was the opening. The boy could reach it with his hands but not his body. He began to panic and pushed forward with all his might. His head almost reached the opening, but he could not move an inch. Chip had trouble breathing as the mountain's weight pressed on his ribcage. He could not move in any direction.

The boy's heart began to beat wildly in fear. He scrambled for the Calm but could not find it. The paralyzing fear made him lose his grip on the Power and the link. The Wall rebuilt itself. The orphan's mind and body screamed in terror. He could not breathe. Vaguely, he heard someone say that Garth was out, and it was Chase's turn. He did not think they knew he was trying to get out on this side.

Chip was all alone.

Suddenly, the trapped boy heard a metallic thud and then a horrendous moan. The Dim was right behind him. Chip, stuck between two slabs of immense rock, became frantic with fright. He heard the scraping of metal on stone as the creature dragged itself towards his wedged body. He could not break through his Wall or seize the Calm. His fear was all-encompassing. Tears filled his eyes.

He was utterly helpless, unable to move.

The life form in the egg suddenly entered his mind. He latched on to it in desperation. It showed him images of blue skies and white clouds, showering him with soothing memories, forcing out all other thoughts. He sank into the images then saw the Calm. Chip wrapped himself in it and looked at his options. He thought he heard that Chase was almost out. The scraping of the Dim sounded right behind him.

He realized he had to do the one thing he feared most. Breathing in as much as he could manage, the boy blew out all the air in his lungs, flattening himself further. Pushing with his toes and grabbing the edge in front of him with his hands, he dragged himself forward, sliding towards the outside world.

Unfortunately, it was still not enough. The opening was too small. At least his arms were out in the night air. Chip's chest was tightly wedged between the rocks, and he could not breathe at all. Strangely calm in that eternal moment, he opened and closed his hands in the open air. The boy felt the Dim reach out and touch the bottom of his foot. It was likely having trouble squeezing between the rocks itself. It was a small measure of comfort. All it had to do was reach a little higher to touch his exposed ankle, and it would all be over.

The life form soothed him.

Trust.

He felt more than heard the word.

"I see his hands!" Princess Eleanor cried, her voice muted.

Chip's mind began to lose consciousness as the air in his lungs ran out. His vision started to fragment around the edges.

Trust.

There was nothing more he could do.

"Pull!" shouted Xander.

Chip felt two strong hands grab his wrists, and at the same time, the Dim seized his foot. He felt tremendous pressure on his arms and the boy's shoulders felt like they would pop out of their sockets. Then pain exploded in his chest and back as he felt his torso drag forward. His foot pulled away from the death grip. Suddenly, Chip's whole body flew out of the crevice onto the mountainside.

He instinctively breathed in hoarse, ragged breaths of fresh mountain air. The others surrounded him while he sat on his rump, inhaling like mad.

"I'm alive!" he finally yelled, laughing with wild abandon. The life form in his side bag beamed happiness. The boy stood up and turned around to see the Dim reaching for the opening, but it could not get through. Its hollow eyes looked at him without expression. His happiness turned to a simmering rage, and he broke through his Wall. Looking around, he assessed his location.

They were halfway up the mountain on its eastern side. Low foothills greeted him as the sun broke over the horizon. He could see the Great Plains stretching forever to the east. He held his awe back as he looked at the others. The boy's eyes blazed a ferocious red, and his voice took on a tone of command.

"Move down the mountain slope," the orphan ordered. "I have one last thing to do."

The weapons master nodded in respect and ushered the others down the slope. Chip followed them a short way, then stopped and waited for them to reach a ridge further down the mountain. He turned to face the Dim. It looked at him, wedged between the two rock slabs, as if challenging him to try to hurt it.

He reached out to the life form in the egg, and the being instantly linked, allowing him full reign of their combined magic. Lifting his hands, the boy unleashed all his pent-up frustration and rage, pulling in more Power than he ever had before, raising his arms to the sky. Above his hands, a fireball formed, the size of which the world had likely never seen.

The immense ball grew and expanded until it extended above the tallest trees. The orphan's hands shook with unimaginable Power, and then with a mighty grunt, he heaved the fireball directly at the Dim. The blazing inferno of flame and destruction struck the side of the mountain in front of the creature with the sound of a hundred thunderstorms. The entire east side of Cave Mountain shuddered then fell in on the Dim. The cavern below the creature filled with crushed stone. Far above it, the rock at the top, now unsupported, gave way.

Half of the mountain fell in on itself, filling the space where the lake rested with the remaining black egg. The stunted top bent and sunk even lower.

The orphan stood on the edge of a vast crater that sloped up towards a new peak. Satisfied, Chip turned to gaze down at his friends, who stood slack-jawed after witnessing such destruction. The damage to the Demon King's lair could not be overestimated.

The rising sun illuminated the boy on the newly created horizon. A mountain wolf's joyous howl sounded in the distance. Chip's eyes blazed bright red as he gazed across the Great Plains, hand resting on the hilt of his sword. To the party gathered below, they could not help but feel hope.

END OF VOLUME 3.

IF YOU ENJOYED READING THIS, please leave a review on Amazon. It would be greatly appreciated.

Visit my website: www.terryironwood.com

Type your email address at the bottom of the page to be notified of my next book launch.

I have added a free short story prequel called "Weapons Master" in the upper right corner of my website. It is Garth Stone's backstory.

The Orphan's Quest audiobook with special effects is now available on Audible.

Link to Volume Four: Guardian

I hope you enjoyed Volume 3: A Dim World. Be sure to look out for Volumes 4 to 7 of The Great Forget Fantasy Series!

The Great Forget Fantasy Series:

Volume 1: Orphan's Quest

Volume 2: Defenders of Hope

Volume 3: A Dim World

Volume 4: Guardian

Volume 5: Wizard's Guild

Volume 6: Stone Kingdom

Volume 7: Coming end of December, 2024.

Acknowledgements

I offer my heartfelt thanks to my family and friends, who provided invaluable support, wisdom, and encouragement. You know who you are. I especially want to mention Kevin C., Steve S., and Ward C., who went above and beyond.

I am delighted to work with my editor, Jason Letts from Imbue Editing, who continues to improve my writing.

Last, and certainly not least, I wish to thank an orphan, Chip, for taking me on his quest.

Many thanks,

Terry Ironwood

ABOUT THE AUTHOR

Terry Ironwood resides with his family. He holds multiple university degrees and is interested in the science of self-improvement. He is equally fascinated with physics and spirituality. Terry believes in an 'attitude of gratitude' and is grateful he can write full-time. His dream is to help others reach their full potential.

Printed in Dunstable, United Kingdom